THRILLERS
and MORE
THRILLERS

Exciting stories of suspense and mystery,
ghosts and the supernatural

THRILLERS
and MORE
THRILLERS

Selected by ROBERT ARTHUR

Illustrations by SAUL LAMBERT

A WINDWARD BOOK

RANDOM HOUSE 🏠 NEW YORK

Windward Books are published by Random House, Inc.
First Windward Silverback Edition, October 1973
Originally published by Random House, Inc., in 1968

Library of Congress Catalog Card Number: 68–23653
ISBN: 0–394–82201–3

Manufactured in the United States of America

The publishers wish to thank the following, for permission to reprint:

Arkham House, Publishers, for "The Calamander Chest," by Joseph Payne Brennan, Copyright 1953 by Weird Tales for "Weird Tales." For "Mrs. Manifold," by Stephen Grendon, Copyright 1949 by Avon Publications, Inc., Copyright 1954 by August Derleth. And for "Mr. George," by August Derleth, Copyright 1946 by Weird Tales for "Weird Tales," Copyright 1953 by August Derleth.

Robert Arthur for "My Displaced Ghosts" by John West, Copyright © 1965 by Robert Arthur.

The Bobbs-Merrill Company, Inc. for "Faith, Hope and Charity" by Irvin S. Cobb from *Faith, Hope and Charity*, Copyright 1934 by Irvin S. Cobb, Renewed 1962 by Laura Baker Cobb.

Miriam Allen deFord, author of "The Poison Necklace," Copyright © 1965 by Davis Publications, Inc.; first published in *Ellery Queen's Mystery Magazine*.

Paul R. Reynolds, Inc. for "The Hands of Mr. Ottermole," by Thomas Burke, Copyright 1931 by Little, Brown & Co., Inc.

Contents

THRILLERS and MORE THRILLERS

Introduction

What is a thriller? It's certainly not just any mystery story, or ghost story, or adventure tale. Any of these can be good stories without being thrillers. On the other hand, a thriller can be any of these.

My own definition is that a thriller is any story that combines suspense and atmosphere in such a way that it becomes more than just a mystery, ghost or adventure story. It may achieve this through an unusual plot, or unusually vivid writing, or a very special background, or all of these qualities. It may be scary, but it doesn't have to be; it can be just unusually suspenseful and interesting of its type.

Probably our greatest writer of thrillers was Edgar Allan Poe. He combined plot, suspense, mood and writing in a way that has seldom, if ever, been equaled. He has been called the father of the mystery story. I think he can be called the spiritual father of the modern thriller. Even though thriller-type stories of ghosts and demons and werewolves and such have been known in folklore for many centuries, Edgar Allan Poe's brooding genius gave us a standard which has influenced other writers ever since.

Just to mention the titles of some of Poe's stories— "The Black Cat," "The Pit and the Pendulum," "The Tell-Tale Heart," "The Murders in the Rue Morgue"— is to evoke a shiver of delighted memory in those who have read them. I have included "The Tell-Tale Heart" as a small sample of Poe's work. If you've read it before you'll enjoy re-reading it. If you're not familiar with Poe, though, and like thrillers, run, don't walk, to the nearest library to get better acquainted with him.

Don't read him for the first time alone at night, though!

It's interesting to wonder what Edgar Allan Poe would be writing if he were alive today. Would he be writing for television? Or would he be writing motion pictures so shuddery the audience could hardly bear to watch?

Perhaps neither. Poe's genius lay in the way he used words to create a mood, an atmosphere, to which the imagination of the reader responds. I think that the best thrillers of all are still those on the printed page, which allow you to paint the pictures to go with the action on the magic canvas of your own imagination.

The other stories in this book are not by Poe, of course. But I hope they will be new to you—and I hope you will enjoy them.

ROBERT ARTHUR
Cape May, N.J. 1968

Mr. George
by AUGUST DERLETH

Now that the sunlight of late afternoon slanted across the lawn, Priscilla took the flowers she had gathered and tied a little blue ribbon around them. She attached the note she had written, clutched the bouquet tightly to her, and tiptoed to the door of her room. She opened it. Voices came up the stairs. But *they* were out in back, and would not hear her leaving the house. If they saw her come back, that would make no difference. She closed the door behind her and marched her sturdy five-year-old self down the carpeted stairs to the front door and outside.

The streetcar conductor recognized her. He bent his moustached face above her and asked, "All alone, Miss Priscilla?"

"Yes, sir."

"It's going on for dark, too. Are you off far?"

"Oh, no. I'm going to see Mr. George."

He looked unhappy. His smile was pale, thin. He said no more.

The streetcar clanged on its way. Priscilla knew that the conductor would tell her just where to get off, but just the same she counted the blocks—the next but one, where Renshaws lived; the one after that, which was Burtons'; the one of vacant lots; and then at last, after three blocks in which no one she knew lived—seven of them in all—the conductor called in that this was her stop.

"Yes, sir. I know. Thank you," she said.

She smiled at him and got off.

He looked after her, troubled; he shook his head. "And what's to become of her with all those vultures around her?" he asked of the mote-ridden air.

All along the way, Priscilla had been a little apprehensive about the big iron gate; but, since it was not yet six o'clock, it stood open. She passed through the open gate and went directly to Mr. George's place. There was nothing to put the flowers in; so she left them there, right where Mr. George would be sure to see them. She was not quite sure about Mr. George. Of late, many things had puzzled her. She did not understand about

Mr. George, nor why he had gone away and left her alone with her mother's cousins, who, she knew with the unerring instinct of a child, did not love her the way Mr. George had loved her, or her mother before him, gone, too.

She pulled out the note and fixed it in such a way that he would be sure to see it. Going away, she looked back several times to see whether he had come; but the flowers lay there undisturbed with the whiteness of the note paper standing out. The flowers were sweet rocket, forget-me-nots, and roses—old-fashioned flowers, the kind Mr. George liked. But Mr. George did not come; he was not in sight when she got to the gate; so, with one last lingering look, she went out into the street and down to the corner to wait for the streetcar, already beginning to wonder whether *they* had missed her.

But, no, they had not. They were still talking when she slipped into the house, though one of them was in the dining room now, and they were all raising their voices a little—not enough to be audible much beyond the front hall. She stood soundless, listening. Though the two women and the man, their brother, were her mother's cousins, Priscilla thought of them as her aunts and uncle. The women were in the kitchen, and Uncle Laban was in the dining room.

Uncle Laban was saying, "The trouble with you, Virginia, is that you have no sense of refinement, no tact. It's just the money you want, and you don't care how you get it."

"It's just *her* who stands between us. You know it as well as I."

"Now that George is gone," said Laban.

"Yes," said Virginia.

There was a nervous titter from Adelaide.

"I often wonder just what was the relation between them?" resumed Virginia. "Were they lovers?"

"It doesn't matter."

"Oh, it does," put in Addie. "If we could prove perhaps that *she* is his child . . ."

Laban made an impatient clucking sound. "Irrelevant and immaterial. Cissie's will is clear, and it makes no difference whether Priscilla is George's or Henry's or even whether she wasn't Cissie's. The will set forth that George was to stay here in Cissie's house until he wished to go . . ."

"Or died," interposed Virginia.

"Don't be unpleasant," said Laban shortly. "And the house, the grounds, and all the money—"

"Three hundred thousand dollars!" sighed Adelaide.

"—belongs to Priscilla."

"You leave out the most important part," said Virginia. "After Priscilla, we come."

"Say, rather, we are here."

"Oh, yes," said Adelaide bitterly, "as we have always been here. On someone's bounty."

"What do you care about that?" asked Laban pettishly. "We have the run of the house—and almost of her bank account."

"I want it openly, aboveboard," said Virginia.

"Oh, you are descending to comedy," said Laban. "But I know you're up to something—letting the servants go one by one."

"They were Cissie's—not mine."

"You haven't replaced any of them."

"No. I'll think about that. Have you got that table done?"

"Yes."

"Go and call her."

Priscilla fled noiselessly up the stairs, so that she would be ready when Uncle Laban called.

On the night side of dusk, Canby, who was on his beat, saw something white fluttering beyond the gate. In the course of routine duty he went in to see what it was. He detached the note, flashed his light around to get such details as might be necessary, and in due course turned the note in at precinct headquarters.

The captain read it.

"Dear Mr. George, please come back. We want you to live with us again. We have plenty of room. You just take the streetcar and go straight east. The house is just like you left it, only now more roses are in bloom."

"No signature?"

"None. It was just there on the grave, with some flowers. I left the flowers. Grave of a man named George Newell. Died about a month ago. Fifty-one years old."

"Looks like a kid's printing. Give it to Orlo Ward— that's the kind of thing he wants for *The New Yorker*."

The old clock in the hall, which had been Grandfather Dedman's, talked all night. Mr. George said that her mother remembered how it talked. It used to say "Cis-sie, Cis-sie, Cis-sie, go-to sleep-now, Cis-sie!" over and over until she went to sleep. Now Priscilla thought it talked to her in the same way. But Priscilla was not sleepy. She lay listening to all the sounds the old house made. She lay mourning her lot, now that the cook—the last one she liked—had been sent away, and the rest of them in the house disliking her. She could tell by the way they looked at her, by the way they talked to her; and there was the feeling she had. If only Mr. George would come back! Nothing had been the way it had always been after her mother went away since the day Mr. George complained he wasn't feeling well and later called her to his bed and said, "Be a good girl now, Priscilla. And remember, if anything goes wrong, go to Laura."—Laura being something to Mr. George as she had been to her mother. But not, like the Lecketts, a blood relative.

The murmur of voices whispered down the hall.

Virginia Leckett was braiding her hair in her brother's room. Laban was already abed.

"And if something did happen to her, there couldn't be any question about our inheriting, could there?" she was asking.

"That's the tenth time you've asked that, I'll swear," he said.

"Could there?" she insisted.

"How? There aren't any other relatives."

"That's what I thought."

"Anyway, she's as healthy as a cow."

"Oh, things could happen."

"What things?"

"You never can tell, Laban."

"You give me the creeps, Virginia."

"Look at the way George went."

"Well, you can't expect Priscilla to develop heart trouble."

"That's what the doctor *said.*"

"That's what he believed, also."

"That could be seen to. There are things that bring on heart attacks."

"You'd better not talk that way, Virginia."

"No?"

"No!"

"Just the same," she went on, talking more rapidly, "if something happened to Priscilla—just think, three hundred thousand dollars! Laban—think what you could do with your share! And I! Why, I could go to Europe."

"But you never would. Why don't you stop torturing yourself about that money? It's out of your reach."

"Is it?"

"You'd better go to your room."

Virginia's footsteps went down the hall, pausing at the door of Priscilla's room. Don't let her come in, God, asked Priscilla with supreme confidence. Virginia went on down the hall, and the hum of voices came distantly from Adelaide's room. It had been this way many nights since Mr. George went away. Sometimes Priscilla would think that she had hated Aunt Virginia the most; but then she would remember Mama telling her never to hate anyone because hate hurts the hater more than the hated—or something like that. Just the same, Priscilla did not trust Aunt Virginia. She did not trust Aunt Adelaide or Uncle Laban, either, but she mistrusted

Aunt Virginia the most. She could not understand what Mama meant when she used to say to Mr. George, "I pity them. They are so narrow, so provincial. When they had money they could have gone to Paris, to Vienna—but no, they had to invest it in shaky stock just to get more, and lost it all. Poor things!"

The clock said, "Pris-sie, Pris-sie, Pris-sie, go-to sleep-now, Pris-sie."

"I'm not sleepy," said Priscilla into the darkness.

The house settled, groaning and creaking. A faucet dripped somewhere, and in the wind outside a limb of the cedar at the northwest corner of the house rapped from time to time against the wall. The clock went on talking, with its loud *tick-tock, tick-tock, tick-tock*. And outside the streetcars clanged past, ever fewer and fewer of them, as the night deepened. Priscilla lay thinking, dreaming almost, of Mama and Mr. George, and of how it had been only a year ago, when they had been where the ocean was, and she had played all day long in the sand, while Mama's cough got worse and worse, and Mr. George grew sad and quiet, and the wind blew, it seemed, colder and colder and blew them at last right back here to the house on Elm Street where Mama had been born. It seemed a long, long time ago, ever so long. Time seemed to stretch out into endless dimensions on every side of her, and she felt lost, lost from Mama and Mr. George, and the sandy beach and all the trains, the strange little coaches of those places far over the ocean, and the ships, and . . .

But now she grew drowsy, and someone came in

through the door and bent over her and whispered, "Go to sleep now, Priscilla."

"All right, Mr. George," she said.

In the morning Priscilla, who was up with the sun, took Celine—the oldest of her dolls, and her favorite, for it had come from Arles, bought by Mama and Mr. George on a lovely holiday from Paris—and went to play in the teahouse at the end of the garden, sitting in the cool shade of the birch trees leaning over. Long before anyone else in the house was out of bed, Priscilla reached her haven with Celine. She was in the habit of carrying on long conversations with Celine, who was pert and quaint at the same time, looking foreign and strange, and, in the circumstances, not too voluble, always saying just the right things.

This morning she was set up in her usual place across from Priscilla, and Priscilla arranged the tea things as she talked. Did Celine have a good night's rest, or were her legs crossed under her again? Would Celine like sugar or lemon or both in her tea, or did Celine prefer to drink it in the proper manner, without anything? The birds sang, for the tree-girt garden was a haven in the midst of the city, and seven blocks was a good flying distance to the trees of the cemetery; so they flew back and forth all day long, and made intimate noises in the shrubbery around the teahouse.

Celine made the appropriate answers.

But there was something strange about her this morning, and presently Priscilla began to look at her as if with new eyes. It seemed to her that Celine was trying very hard to say something to her—something really original, that did not come from Priscilla first. "Take care," she seemed to say. "Watch out."

Priscilla looked around her in momentary alarm, so real did Celine's voice seem. But there was no one there.

"Watch out for whom?" she asked in a whisper.

"For *them!*" said Celine. But what an odd voice for a doll's, thought Priscilla.

Then she looked very covertly around her on all sides of the teahouse. She knew that voice! She did, indeed. It was Mr. George's—and it was just like him to pretend it was Celine's.

She clapped her hands and cried out gaily, "Come out, come out, wherever you are, Mr. George."

No one came.

"Please, Mr. George."

A mourning dove cooed.

"Don't tease me."

No answer.

She looked at Celine, but the doll was as bland as ever. She looked away, over her shoulder.

"Watch out," said Celine in Mr. George's voice.

She whirled, looking this way and that. "I'll find you," she cried out. "I will, I will!" She darted into the bushes, peering this way and that, with such violence that the birds were still, save for a blue jay who sent out warning cries about her intrusion to every part of the garden.

"Whatever is that child doing?" inquired Adelaide from the window.

"What?" asked Virginia, hooking herself into her old-fashioned dress before the mirror.

"Why, running around and around the teahouse. She seems to be looking for something. Or someone."

"Children have imaginary playmates."

"It's crazy, Ginny. Now, I wonder!"

Virginia looked at her. Sometimes that too-large head on that short, thin body produced an idea of merit, from Virginia's point of view. "What is it now, Addie?"

Adelaide looked at her out of narrowed eyes. "Do you suppose it might be possible to have her declared—well, not insane, exactly—but . . ."

"Oh, no, that would never do. There are so many other ways. A slow poison, for instance."

"Don't be crude, Virginia," said Laban from the threshold. "For God's sake, are we going to have breakfast? If you insist on firing the cook, somebody in this household ought to be ready to assume kitchen responsibilities."

"We're coming," said Virginia. "Do see what Priscilla's doing."

Laban crossed to the window and looked out.

After a while he said, "She appears to be holding a conversation."

"Oh, yes, with the doll. I've noticed that," said Virgina.

"No, not with the doll."

"Not? Is she alone?"

"Yes. Her back's to the doll; she's not even looking at it."

Virginia turned. "Adelaide, will you go out and call

her in for breakfast?" And, when Adelaide had gone, she said to Laban, "I don't like to be called 'crude', Laban."

He shrugged. He had been thinking about what he might inherit if anything did happen to Priscilla; Virginia had planted seed in fertile ground. "Don't be, then," he said. "What do you suppose people would think if she died like that? After all, the terms of Cissie's will aren't a dead secret. There would be questions. Finally, poison can be traced—even the most obscure poison, which you wouldn't get hold of, anyway."

"If you can think of anything better, why don't you?"

"It would have to be an accident of some kind—or at least, look like one. Only the other day I read something in the *Sun* about an accident which took the lives of two children. Playing in the attic, locking themselves into a trunk. They were suffocated. That could so easily happen, you know. How could anyone prove differently? But poison involves certain chemical and physiological factors which are incapable of being made to tell a story different from the facts."

Adelaide came back, a little breathless. "Imaginary playmates, is it? She says George is out there somewhere, hiding from her. She says he talked to her."

Virginia smiled. "That is putting her innermost wish into a fantasy she can live. It's the height of imagination. What did he say?"

"She didn't tell me."

"Is she in?"

"She's coming."

"We shall see."

Priscilla came in and sat down at the table. It was not set. She waited, looking at the three of them—Uncle Laban, fat, jolly-looking except for his soft, full mouth and his small dark eyes; Aunt Adelaide with her grotesquely fat head, so heavy that it always lolled a little; Aunt Virginia with her thin line of mouth and her hard blue eyes. All were dressed in black—Adelaide in taffeta, Virginia in brocade, Laban in broadcloth. All were now busy in some fashion or other—Laban with the morning paper, Adelaide scurrying about to set the table, Virginia at getting breakfast.

It was hard for Priscilla to sit still, because she was convinced that Mr. George had slipped into the house with her, and was even now concealed somewhere in the room. Her eyes darted inquisitively this way and that; momentarily she expected him to reveal himself. But nothing happened, and meanwhile Adelaide had brought all the dishes and then at last came with Virginia bearing eggs and bacon and toast, and a glass of milk for Priscilla. All sat down, Laban putting his paper aside.

"With whom were you talking in the teahouse, Priscilla?" asked Virginia.

"With Celine," answered Priscilla around her glass of milk, which she had begun to drink.

"Who else?" asked Laban.

No answer.

"I asked you, who else?"

Priscilla shook her head.

"You told *me,*" said Adelaide.

"Mr. George," said Priscilla.

"Indeed! And what did he say?" asked Virginia.

Priscilla shook her head again.

"Answer me."

Priscilla remained silent.

Virginia turned to the others. "You see, it's imagination."

"He came back last night. I asked him to," said Priscilla.

Adelaide tittered. Virginia flashed her a quick, angry glance. Laban hawked and bent to his bacon and eggs.

There were no more questions. Each of them was thinking his own thoughts. Priscilla still hoped secretly for Mr. George to pop up and surprise them all. Adelaide thought of the way in which children played by themselves. Virginia contemplated the three of them alone in the house—*their* house—without Priscilla. Laban thought there was no good in delaying matters; accidents did not wait upon auspicious moments. Besides, the concept of a hundred thousand dollars which might be his to do with as he liked had grown immeasurably and now loomed directly before his mind's eye as a vast mountain of epitomized freedom, opening the world to him as it had never been open before.

Finishing his breakfast, he gazed at Priscilla, who had also finished, and smiled. "Where did George go?" he asked.

She was disarmed. "I think he's hiding."

"I'll bet I know where he's hiding," continued Laban. "Should we go and look?"

"Oh, yes, let's."

Laban pushed his chair away and got up. "Come along, then."

"Excuse me," said Priscilla to the two women.

They went out into the hall, Priscilla clinging to his hand.

"I know just where he would be," said Laban, leading the way to the stairs.

"Upstairs?"

"In the attic. It's dark there."

The dimness of the attic resolved itself for Laban into a giant funnel at the end of which loomed the partly-filled steamer trunk not far from the top of the attic stairs. He began to circle the outer edge of the funnel, moving things and looking behind them. Priscilla darted here and there, but every few moments she stood quite still and asked questioningly of the musty twilight, "Mr. George?"

"We'll find him," said Laban each time, with a nervous heartiness. His hands were clammy, and cold sweat started to his forehead as he drew nearer and nearer to the trunk.

The trunk was large and very heavy; once inside, it would be quite impossible for Priscilla to lift the lid, even if the hasp were not caught. All the darkness of the attic, which was large and reached into the gables of the old house, seemed to converge upon the trunk. Twice Priscilla stopped almost beside it.

"He isn't here," said Priscilla at last.

"I'll bet he is," said Laban. "There's one more place just big enough to hide him. Right there."

He bent and lifted the heavy lid. The trunk was almost as deep as Priscilla was tall, though the things still packed in it diminished its depth a little. He looked at the child from the corners of his eyes; she seemed entranced, standing almost on tiptoe to peer toward the dark maw of the trunk.

"That's too dark for me to see him even if he is there," said Laban. "Maybe he's hidden under the clothes. Crawl in and find him, Pris."

Priscilla took two steps forward and heard someone say, "No, Priscilla."

"Oh!" she exclaimed, clasping her hands. "It's Mr. George!"

"What?" Laban was startled.

"He's here somewhere. I heard him."

Laban gazed at her with amazed wonder at the vividness of her imagination. Then he said, "I'll bet he's hidden under this clothing. Just crawl in and surprise him, Pris."

She shook her head. "Mr. George says not to."

A kind of exasperation was growing in him. He came down to his knees beside the trunk. "See," he said, "I'll prop up the lid." He pushed a heavy book upright between the lid and the trunk. "I'll be right here in case he comes out."

Priscilla shook her head. "You look," she said.

He thought quickly. If she could be persuaded to stand beside him, it would be simple to tip her into the trunk without any kind of rough handling which might later show a bruise on the delicate flesh.

"Come and help me," he said, bending to peer into the darkness.

Priscilla came forward.

Just short of him something stopped her, something like an invisible hand pressing her back. Something tall and dark took shadowy shape beside Laban where he knelt, waiting for her, something that reached down and tore the sustaining book from beneath the trunk-lid, something that pushed the trunk-lid down with weighty impact upon Laban Leckett's neck.

He gave a choking cry, humped up horribly, and collapsed, kicking a little.

"Go away, Priscilla. Go downstairs now."

"Yes, Mr. George."

Priscilla went obediently out of the attic, down the stairs, and back to the teahouse, where she sat and told Celine all about it, very animated.

At the window stood Virginia, looking out with narrowed eyes and a derisive smile on her face. "I knew it," she said over her shoulder to Adelaide. "There never was much man about Laban. He lost his nerve."

On the day after the funeral, Laura Craig came to call. Like the Leckett women, Laura Craig was in her fifties, but she looked considerably younger. She dressed well, having money and knowing how to use it, knowing it was only a means to an end, not an end in itself. She had been a beautiful woman, and was still a strikingly handsome one; in appearance there was the difference of day and night between her and her hostesses, Laura being colorful and jeweled as against their almost offensive plainness.

"I was shocked to read about Laban," she said without preamble. "I read it only this morning. I've been up in Connecticut, and I am sorry to have missed the services. However did such a thing happen?"

"The lid of the trunk was very heavy," said Virginia, quick to speak before Adelaide could say anything. "I suppose Laban was careless."

"How dreadful!" exclaimed Laura. "But what was he looking for?"

Virginia shrugged, and raised her eyebrows.

"Something of Father's, we think," said Adelaide. "That was Father's trunk, you know. The last time it was used was when Father went to the Exposition in St. Louis."

"It was only by accident that we found him," added Virginia. "We just missed him finally, and went to look for him. He had been dead quite a while. It was awful—the trunk-lid came down with such force that it almost severed his head. We have destroyed the trunk, naturally."

"I should think so," said Laura.

The talk drifted politely toward Priscilla, and presently Priscilla herself was walking down to the front gate with Laura Craig, whom she also called "Aunt." The sisters Leckett stood behind the curtains at the windows to make sure that Priscilla did not linger too long with this woman, who they knew had come primarily to assure herself that the child was all right.

"Let us hope she says nothing of her absurd fancies to *her*," said Virginia bitterly.

"You forbade her to speak of them again."

"Oh, I know—but children recognize no restrictions. Will she ever forget George Newell? I wonder."

"It won't make any difference, will it?" Adelaide tittered.

"Be still, Adelaide." She sighed. "What *could* have happened up there? Laban was never careless!"

"You know what she said."

"Oh, Addie! A farrago of shadows and George and nonsense! Are you thinking the house is haunted by George? How laughable!"

Adelaide sniffed a little and left the window.

"It can't be denied, however, that Laban's death leaves each of us richer by fifty thousand dollars—after Priscilla, that is."

"How can you say such a thing, Addie!" said Virginia sharply.

Adelaide turned. "How can I say what?"

"What you just said about Laban's death."

"I didn't say anything about Laban's death."

Virginia turned angrily. "Why, Addie! I heard you. Don't try to deny it."

"Are you out of your mind, Ginny? I haven't opened my mouth. What did you imagine you heard now?"

"You said we would each be richer by fifty thousand dollars as a result of Laban's death."

"Why, I never!"

"You did!"

"I did not! That, if anything, is a thought which would occur to you a long time before I would think of it." Thoughtfully, she added, "It's true, though, isn't it?"

Virginia said nothing. Something gnawed persistently at her consciousness; it was the knowledge that if something were to happen to Adelaide before Priscilla died, she, Virginia, would come into three hundred thousand dollars, without the need of sharing it with anyone at all. A little shaken, she forgot about Priscilla and Laura Craig out in the afternoon sun at the gate and came away from the window. She was caught in a mesh of greed and conflicting desires.

The cedar limb tapped against the house once for every five times the old clock in the hall said *tick-tock*. Priscilla counted in the dark, and communicated her findings to Celine, whom she had permitted to share her bed that night. She set herself next to counting the times the faucet dripped. But this, she found, was next to impossible, for the drippings were never very certain or clear. And there were other sounds alive in the dark in the old house. The attic shutter was loose; it creaked and banged in the wind. Something rustled down the hall, and Priscilla knew it was Aunt Adelaide again; in a few moments voices made a murmuring sound which joined the voices of the night.

In her sister's room, Adelaide walked nervously beside the bed. "It's no use your telling me it's my imagination, Virginia. I know I saw something. This is the third time, and I never heard that hallucinations come in threes."

"And what was it this time? Try to be coherent, Addie."

"A shadow, in the hall, at the head of the stairs."

"If you weren't so vain about your eyes, I think an oculist and a pair of spectacles would lay your shadow."

"I stood still. The shadow moved. It was a man. I want to get out of this house. I hate it! I've hated it all my life—since we had to come and live here as Cissie's 'guests'."

"So do I. Just be patient, Addie. It takes time."

"Yes, always waiting!" She turned and bent over Virginia, instinctively lowering her voice. "I've thought of something. You know what Laban said about accidents. I've watched her swing. That's an awfully heavy swing, and when George made it for her he reinforced the oak seat with iron. If she should jump too soon and not get out of the way quickly enough—and if it should catch her somehow . . . I think it could happen."

"Or be made to happen," added Virginia softly. "Think of that now, Addie, instead of absurd hallucinations. And for heaven's sake, don't tell anyone you think you see men on the stairs—you know what people would think!"

Grandfather Dedman's clock said, "Pris-sie, Pris-sie, Pris-sie, go-to sleep-now, Pris-sie." This time the cedar limb tapped on "sleep." Priscilla snuggled deeper into her bed and turned to Celine.

"Are you sleepy, Celine?" she asked.

Celine obligingly indicated that she was not.

Aunt Adelaide rustled back down the hall to her own room. Priscilla knew that her aunts had things to say to each other they did not want her to hear. She wondered sometimes what it might be they talked about, but she did not mind their ignoring her. No more did she care to have them listen to her conversations with Celine. Or with Mr. George.

She raised up on her elbows and peered into the darkness of the room. Little light came in from outside; the close-pressing trees shut away all but two small rays of the street lights; one of these struck the opposite wall near the door, the other hit the mirror, where it reflected like a dim opening to a remote world of day.

"Mr. George, are you there?" she whispered into the darkness.

"Yes, Priscilla."

The answer came, it seemed, from all around her and from inside her at the same time. She did not question it.

"Please come where I can see you."

A part of the darkness near the door detached itself and drifted toward her bed; it crossed the light but did not shut it away from the mirror or the door; it left no shadow because it was itself a shadow. It hovered over the bed, and settled down to one side of it, sitting there. It was not strange to Priscilla. She was comforted.

"Say good night to Mr. George, Celine," she said.

Clad in her negligee, Laura Craig wrote to George Newell's brother in London, the hour being late and everything still. She wrote swiftly. The words came easily, for they had been pent up so long. . .

". . . I think there is no question but that Priscilla is George's child. She has his look about her eyes; that was not so noticeable a short time ago, but now it is coming out. And she is constantly obsessed with him. I do not know that that is good. Surely George would not think so if he were still alive, though he was absolutely devoted to her, as you know; so many of us thought that was because of Cissie and her slow dying. What is important, I think, is that some way ought to be found to take Priscilla away from the Lecketts. They are definitely nineteenth century, and they have that kind of repressive way of life which is actually more wicked and evil than sheer wantonness. I mean that they certainly always resented being pitied by Cissie and even her goodness, which they never deserved. They are *not* good for Priscilla, though I found her remarkably self-contained, which is probably because she is left alone so very much. That is not good, either, I think you will agree. She has found time to think up the strangest fancies. For instance, she believes that George is still in the house. She says that George pushed the trunk-lid down on Laban's neck. That is absurd, of course; it is the wildest of fancies—but from all I have heard, the lid did more damage to Laban's neck than it ought to have done, if it fell under its own power. There is something very strange about all this, and it will come as no surprise to you to learn that I have begun to wonder a little about George's death, too. After all, his heart wasn't *that* bad. I saw him only three days before he died, and he said then that his condition seemed somewhat improved by sedentary living. I have to admit that my impression of the Lecketts is of the worst—I think they are selfish, greedy, lazy, and evil people, who, behind their old-fashioned respectability, are capable of absolutely anything . . ."

The summer deepened, and as it grew more sultry, Priscilla spent still more of her time in the yard. Her routine in the morning was unvaried. She went to the teahouse before breakfast, and returned to it afterward. Sometimes she received little notes and presents from Laura Craig, after which she was plagued by questions from Aunt Virginia and Aunt Adelaide. Priscilla could not know that the women were anxious to learn whether she had told Laura Craig anything; Priscilla, failing to understand the real goals of their innocuous questions, did not say. She fenced with them unconsciously, thwarting them. Though she did not understand, she was conscious of a feeling of dislike for her in them; but this did not trouble her, as long as they inflicted no punishment beyond the meanness of their words or actions upon her.

In the afternoon she worked in her own little garden, which the women had allowed her to keep in one corner. And later, she retreated to the heavily shaded portion of the walled lawn where the swing hung from the limb of an ancient oak tree. She could swing for hours; from the top of the arc she made, she could look out into the street and once in a while she could see the streetcar going by. Swinging gave her a sense of wild freedom; swinging made her feel that she had escaped the house and the women, that she was back in a world of green trees and sun and sky and birds, like that lovely lost time in Paris and Sorrento and on the beaches in Florida, when they had all three still been together— Mama and Mr. George and she. She never tired of pumping with her sturdy little legs until she was high enough to see, and she was glad that no one ever told her to stop. Once in a while, too, Aunt Adelaide had come out to push her, which was even better.

That August afternoon Aunt Adelaide came out again.

"Today I will jump from higher yet," said Priscilla.

She had learned, under Aunt Adelaide's urging, how much fun it was to leap from the careening swing, to fly through the air, as it were, under her own power.

Aunt Adelaide smiled.

It was a day of clouds, with rain impending. The birds were still, and Celine sat sedately forgotten in the tea-house. There was no wind, and the oak leaves drooped with wonderful pungence over that corner of the lawn, shutting out most of the sky, protecting them from the curious eyes of neighbors.

"I will jump from so high," said Priscilla.

"No, that's too high."

"I can do it, Aunt Adelaide."

"No, Priscilla, that is too high. You might break a leg or something. Just think, six feet."

Priscilla was insistent. "I can so jump from that high."

"No," said Aunt Adelaide shortly. "You may jump only from so high."

"But I jumped from that high the last time."

"Just the same, that's high enough."

Adelaide had calculated very carefully. Priscilla jumped in a kind of crouch; then she straightened up and began to run back to get into the swing again. If she were halted at just the right place in that run

back, and her attention distracted, the swing would
catch her on the back of the head with deadly force.
Because Priscilla reminded her of Cissie, whom she had
always envied as a girl because of her beauty, so much in
contrast to Adelaide's over-sized head, Adelaide hated
Priscilla. It seemed to her the most important thing in
the world to do something to that lovely little head,
because somehow she would be doing something to that
even lovelier head which had been Cissie's; obscurely
she would achieve a kind of compensation for the ab-
normality of her own. It was far more important than
the money which meant so much to Virginia.

"At least, to begin with, that's high enough,"
amended Aunt Adelaide.

"I'll jump later, then."

"We shall see. Come, get in."

Priscilla climbed into the swing and Adelaide began
to push her slowly, steadily. The swing's arc increased.
Now Priscilla could see level with the top of the wall;
now she could see over; now she was well up in the hot
August air, almost brushing the leaves, taking deep
breaths of the oak's perfume each time she came up
under the leaves. And the streetcar was coming, *clang-
clang* at the corner, and up toward the house; she would
see it from both ends of the arc. She always hoped that
the conductor would see her, so that she could wave to
him; but he never did. The limbs and the leaves
were too thick, and he never looked up much from the
tracks.

Adelaide stopped pushing her and stepped back a
little.

"Stay sitting now," she said.

"I am," said Priscilla.

The swing began to slow down, the arc to diminish. She came down from the leafy sky, she came down out of heaven each time a little more. She came away from a pewee singing up in the oak tree, back toward Aunt Adelaide waiting to catch the swing as soon as she had jumped.

"I'm going to jump now."

"Not yet."

She waited a moment.

"Now, then."

"Not yet."

She waited another of the diminishing arcs.

"Now," she said, and jumped, throwing up her arms like a bird, and like a white bird flying to the ground, coming down in a supple crouch and bounding to her feet.

"Oh, fun!" she cried and turned to run to Aunt Adelaide, who stood with the swing held high over her head.

"Oh, look—a redbird!" cried Aunt Adelaide, pointing toward the wall.

Priscilla stopped and turned quickly.

With all her strength, Adelaide pushed the heavy swing. The curve was right; it would catch Priscilla on the back of the head just past the lowest point of the arc; it would crush and mangle forever that lovely head which was so like Cissie's. She took three steps forward, the simulated cry of horror already rising in her throat . . . and faltered.

The swing stopped short of Priscilla's head.

Caught in a dark, gangling shadow that seemed to depend from the tree, the swing went swiftly up and vanished into the oak. Then it came hurtling down with incredible force, clear of Priscilla, straight at Adelaide. Fear rooted her there directly in its path. The heavy, iron-reinforced board struck her across the temple; she dropped without a sound, while the child still looked in vain for the bird.

Priscilla turned and saw the woman crumpled there.

"Aunt Adelaide!" she cried.

Aunt Virginia came running from the house, crying, "Addie! Addie!"

"Go to your room, Priscilla."

The voice came in the whisper of the oak leaves, where a wind was starting up; it rose out of the shadowed heart of the tree and descended all about her like a cloak, as if to shut away the mangled head and the blood there, and the sight of Aunt Virginia like a madwoman coming to her knees beside Adelaide's body.

"All right, Mr. George," said Priscilla.

After Priscilla was in bed, Aunt Virginia came into the room. She came over and sat down beside her on the bed. The undertaker had come and gone a long time ago, and some men from a newspaper had been and gone, too.

"Tell me how it happened now, Priscilla."

"I don't know."

"Why are you so stubborn?"

"I don't know. She said to look at the redbird. I tried

to see it. I couldn't. When I turned around, she was on the ground."

"What else?"

"Nothing, except that Mr. George told me to go to my room."

"George?"

"Yes."

"Did you see him?"

"No."

"No what?"

"No, Aunt Virginia."

"How do you know it was George?"

"I know."

"How?"

"I heard him." She spoke resentfully, not understanding why Aunt Virginia pressed her so. "Besides, Mr. George talks to me every night before I go to sleep."

Aunt Virginia looked grim and pale. Her lips were twitching a little at one corner and her eyes were narrowed. Her hands were clenched on her knees. Deep within her there was a trembling of fear, an insistent awareness which she pushed back with fierce determination.

"You are a wicked little girl," said Aunt Virginia. "What does he say?"

Priscilla, hurt, shook her head.

"Answer me."

Priscilla said nothing.

"Priscilla!"

No answer.

Baffled and angry, Virginia got up and walked out of the room, turning the light switch at the door.

Priscilla waited until she was sure the woman had gone; then she got up in the darkness and found her doll. She returned to bed with it, and tucked Celine in. Then she tiptoed to the door and opened it a little. Aunt Virginia had gone downstairs; a faint scratching sound rose to Priscilla's listening ears. Aunt Virginia was writing something; but of course, she would be writing all about Adelaide. Priscilla closed the door soundlessly and tiptoed back to her bed, crawling in and snuggling close to Celine.

All the intimate sounds of the old house crept into the room, bringing their tranquility. Swinging always made Priscilla tired, and even though she had not been swung as much as usual that afternoon, she was still tired. She drowsed, but she did not sleep. She waited confidently for Mr. George to come.

Having finished her letter, Virginia Leckett put out the lamp and stood for a moment to accustom herself to the darkness. Then she went up the stairs without light. She paused at Priscilla's door.

What was it within? Voices or a voice?

She listened.

"Why don't you ever come where I can see you plainer, Mr. George?"

Virginia heard no answer.

"Do you sleep there by the door, Mr. George?"

No sound.

"All right, Mr. George."

Thereafter, silence.

Noiselessly, Virginia opened the door and looked into the room. The bed was spectral over near the window, and the child dark in it. Darkness filled the room—and yet more dark. Was it an accident of sight that she seemed to see a dark shadow hulking there beside the bed? Yes? Or no? Virginia stared. The intensity of her gaze tricked her; the rays of light from the street seemed to dance; they shone through the shadow beside the bed. Virginia closed her eyes and held her lids down; then she flashed them open. Nothing had changed.

She withdrew, closing the door and standing with her back against it.

In a moment she was sharply, frighteningly aware of menace beyond the door, a potent danger threatening her. It was intangible, but all the more frightening for that intangibility. She started away from the door to stand in the middle of the hall. She took hold of herself, grimly. She was too close to her goal now to be frightened by her imagination. She came back to the door once again, pressing against it with the length of her body. There was something beyond it, something lurking there, waiting. She clenched her hands in a gesture of defiance and moved away to her own room.

There she sat for a long time trying to think what it was that had seized hold of her imagination so vividly, trying to piece together the events of Priscilla's world, thinking always of the insistent fact that, now that Adelaide was gone, she alone would inherit three hundred thousand dollars as soon as Priscilla was gone. That was the world, that was independence, security, freedom for life.

It was late when they came back from the funeral. Virginia had thriftily engaged a car to take them to the cemetery, but not to bring them back. They came back on the streetcar. Laura Craig's presence at the services had vexed Virginia, so that she was unusually short with Priscilla. She recognized that Laura would have liked control over Priscilla; she knew that Laura was genuinely fond of the child, and she resented this —not because of any feeling of possession, but simply because she knew that when something happened to Priscilla, Laura Craig would put people up to asking questions. It was a wonder she had not done so about George Newell.

As she stepped into the hall in the late afternoon, Virginia thought she saw someone standing at the foot of the stairs; but at that moment Priscilla darted forward with a little cry, and she followed her with her eyes where she ran for the stairs and up. When she looked back, there was nothing there. Nevertheless, she was troubled by the increasing frequency of what could only be illusions.

She put away her good coat and hat, and went out into the kitchen to put together something for the supper table. In the routine of getting a meal, she forgot about her illusions, and thought only about how long she must wait before she could take care of Priscilla and enter upon that new world of her dreams.

Priscilla came in, divested of her good clothes and plainly attired in a print dress.

"Didn't you see him, Aunt Virginia?" she cried.

"See whom?"

"Mr. George. He was really and truly standing there when we came in."

Virginia prevented herself from striking the child just in time. She stood looking at her coldly for a long time before she could bring herself to speak. "I never want to hear his name again, do you understand?"

"Yes, Aunt Virginia."

"I never want it mentioned in this house again, do you hear?"

"Yes, Aunt Virginia. You don't have to scream."

"I'm not screaming!"

Her voice screamed back at her from the walls, shrill, raucous, unpleasant, until the sound diminished and faded into the kitchen's silence, which lay like a mountain between the child with her curious bright eyes, and the angry, frightened woman.

The summer passed, and autumn came with rain.

In October, Virginia Leckett could contain herself no longer. Her patience had worn thin. Even the need of showing some superficial concern for Priscilla was becoming increasingly difficult, especially when she thought of how only this child stood between her and the fortune which, by now, she had convinced herself should have been hers all along.

She had evolved a plan for what must be Priscilla's fatal accident. It was not original. She had observed that the child was in the habit of running along the upper hall and down the stairs, despite their steepness. It should be a very simple matter to fix a thin wire across the head of the stairs, half a foot or so from the floor; Priscilla could not possibly avoid tripping over it.

The tumble down the stairs might not kill her, but the chances were good that it would.

She waited one night until Priscilla had gone to her room. Then she went quickly to the head of the stairs and fixed the wire around the posts there, and, stepping over it, hastened to the foot of the stairs.

"Priscilla!" she called. "Come down here—quick!"

From where she stood, she could make out the thin wire because a little light struck up toward it from below. It would be invisible to Priscilla.

The door of Priscilla's room opened. "Did you call me, Aunt Virginia?"

"Yes. Come down, quick."

She came running down the hall.

Virginia stood open-mouthed, watching, a kind of bestial eagerness stirring within her.

But at the head of the stairs Priscilla stopped. A kind of shuddering horror chilled Virginia, for she saw a familiar dark shadow holding the child back with one tenuous arm, while with the other it unwound the wire from the posts. Only when it had been pulled away from Priscilla's path was she permitted to go on.

Down she came.

"What's the matter, Aunt Virginia?"

Virginia's tongue was thick. "I told you—to come—quick. What kept you?"

"*He* did."

"Who?"

"You know who. You said not to mention his name again."

A harsh burst of laughter broke from Virginia's dry

lips. She reached down and took the child by the hand.

"Come along," she said. "We'll see."

She went up the stairs, forcing herself, driving herself every step of the way, so that Priscilla walked always a little ahead of her. They went directly to Priscilla's room. Virginia stopped at the threshold.

"There is nobody here but us," she said. "Do you see?"

Priscilla looked around. "He can hide anywhere," she said.

Virginia shook her. "Do you hear me? There is nobody here but us. Say that after me."

"You're hurting me."

"Say it!" said Virginia in a furious voice.

"There is nobody here but us," repeated Priscilla, frightened now.

"There is nobody in this house but us," Virginia went on, her voice rising. "Say it. Go on—say it."

"There is nobody in this house but us," said Priscilla. She took a deep breath and added courageously, "And Mr. George."

In an excess of thwarted rage, Virginia beat Priscilla unmercifully until the child escaped her and ran to hide under the bed. Breathing heavily, Virginia left the room, slamming the door, and leaning against it to listen. Only the child's sobbing came into the darkness of the hall.

"Are you ready, Virginia?"

She whirled.

Standing almost near enough to touch her was a dark something that spoke to her in George Newell's voice—a horrible sentient darkness without substance but exuding a malignance great enough to send her pulse high in terror. The malign shadow reached toward her.

She screamed and burst away.

She ran faster than she had ever run before toward the stairs.

Too late, she saw that the wire was back in place. She tripped and hurtled down the stairs like a rag doll, while the shadow paused to unwind the wire once again.

Priscilla, after a few moments of uncertainty, came to the threshold of her room and stood in the open doorway.

"Aunt Virginia?" she asked of the darkness.

"Priscilla."

"Yes, Mr. George."

"Priscilla, go to Laura. Tell her Aunt Virginia fell downstairs and broke her neck. You are going to stay with Laura now."

"Yes, Mr. George. Are you coming, too?"

"No. I'm going away, and this time I'll stay. Unless you need me."

"Oh, don't go, Mr. George!"

"Get your things and go to Laura, Priscilla."

Obediently she went back to her room and got Celine out of bed. She put on Celine's hat and then her own. Grandfather Dedman's clock said, "Pris-sie, Pris-sie, Pris-sie, go-to sleep-now, Pris-sie," and then struck ten somber bongs which rang through the house like a tocsin.

Priscilla went out of the room and down the stairs,

walking carefully around Aunt Virginia, expecting that any moment that horrible inert mass might spring up and beat her again. At the front door she turned and looked bravely back into the darkness.

"Good by, Mr. George," she said.

She thought there was an answer, but she could not be sure. Perhaps it was just Grandfather Dedman's clock with a last, reproachful "Pris-sie."

She got on the streetcar at the corner.

"Are you alone, Miss Priscilla?" asked the conductor. "At this time of night?"

"Yes, sir."

"Did you run away?"

"Oh no. I've got to go somewhere else." Gravely, she told him the address.

"Why, that's way over on the other side of the city! What can she be thinking of to let you go alone!"

Irate, he clanged a passing taxi to a stop, got out with Priscilla and put her into it, giving the driver explicit directions.

Laura Craig, white-faced, listened to Priscilla, and, having heard, went directly to the telephone. She called the Leckett house.

Priscilla heard the ringing for a long time. But, of course, there was no answer. So she knew that Mr. George was gone, too, like all the rest of them.

The Calamander Chest
by JOSEPH PAYNE BRENNAN

"From the Indies, sir!" said the second-hand dealer, pressing his palms together. "Genuine calamander wood—a rare good buy, sir!"

"Well—I'll take it," replied Ernest Maax somewhat hesitantly.

He had been strolling idly through the antique and secondhand shop when the chest caught his attention. It had a rich, exotic look which pleased him. In appearance the dark brown, black-striped wood resembled ebony. And the chest was quite capacious. It was at least two feet wide and five feet long, with a depth of nearly three feet. When Maax learned that the dealer was willing to dispose of it for only twelve dollars, he could not resist buying it.

What made him hesitate a little was the dealer's initial low price and quite obvious pleasure upon completing the transaction. Was that fine-grained wood only an inlay or did the chest contain some hidden defect?

When it was delivered to his room the next day, he could find nothing wrong with it. The calamander wood was solid and sound and the entire chest appeared to be in fine condition. The lid clicked smoothly into place when lowered, and the big iron key turned readily enough.

Feeling quite satisfied with himself, Maax carefully polished the dark wood and then slid the chest into an empty corner of his room. The next time he changed his lodgings, the chest would prove invaluable. Meanwhile it added just the right exotic touch to his rather drab chamber.

Several weeks passed, and although he still cast occasional admiring glances at his new possession, it gradually began to recede from his mind.

Then one evening his attention was returned to it in a very startling manner. He was sitting up, reading, late in the evening, when for some reason his eyes lifted from his book and he looked across the room toward the corner where he had placed the chest.

A long white finger protruded from under its lid.

He sat motionless, overwhelmed with sudden horror, his eyes riveted on this appalling object.

It just hung there unmoving, a long pale finger with a heavy knuckle bone and a black nail.

After his first shock, Maax felt a slow rage kindling within him. The finger had no right to be there; it was unreasonable—and idiotic. He resented it bitterly, much as he would have resented the sudden intrusion of an unsavory roomer from down the hall. His peaceful, comfortable evening was ruined by this outrageous manifestation.

With an oath, he hurled his book straight at the finger.

It disappeared. At least he could no longer see it. Tilting his reading light so that its beams shot across the room, he strode to the chest and flung open the lid.

There was nothing inside.

Dropping the lid, he picked up his book and returned to the chair. Perhaps, he reflected, he had been reading too much lately. His eyes, in protest, might be playing tricks on him.

For some time longer he pretended to read, but at frequent intervals he lifted his eyes and looked across the room toward the calamander chest. The finger did not reappear and eventually he went to bed.

A week passed and he began to forget about the finger. He stayed out more during the evening, and read less, and by the end of a week he was quite convinced that he had been the victim of nothing more than an odd hallucination brought on by simple eye strain.

At length, at the beginning of the second week, deciding that his eyes had had a good rest, he bought some current magazines and made up his mind to spend the evening in his room.

Some time after he took up the first magazine, he glanced over at the chest and saw that all was as it should be. Settling comfortably in his chair, he became absorbed in the magazine and did not put it aside for over an hour. As he finally laid it down and prepared to pick up another, his eyes strayed in the direction of the chest—and there was the finger.

It hung there as before, motionless, with its thick knuckle and repulsive black nail.

Crowding down an impulse to rush across the room, Maax slowly reached over to a small table which stood near his chair and felt for a heavy metal ash tray. As his hand closed on the tray, his eyes never left the finger.

Rising very slowly, he began to inch across the room. He was certain that the ash tray, if wielded with force, would effectively crush anything less substantial than itself which it descended on. It was made of solid metal, and it possessed a sharp edge.

When he was a scant yard away from the chest, the finger disappeared. When he lifted the lid, the chest, as he had expected, was empty.

Feeling considerably shaken, he returned to his chair and sat down. Although the finger did not reappear, he could not drive its hideous image out of his mind. Before going to bed, he reluctantly decided that he would get rid of the chest.

He was in sound health and his eyes had had a week's rest. Therefore, he reasoned, whatever flaw in nature permitted the ugly manifestation rested not with him but with the chest itself.

Looking back, he recalled the secondhand dealer's eagerness to sell the chest at a ridiculously low price. The thing must already have had an evil reputation when the antique dealer acquired it. Knowing it, the unscrupulous merchant had readily consented to part with it for a small sum.

Maax, a practical young man, admitted the possibility of a non-physical explanation only with reluctance, but felt that he was not in a position to debate the matter. The preservation of stable nerves came first. All other considerations were secondary.

Accordingly, on the following day, before leaving for work, he arranged with his landlady to have the chest picked up and carted off to the city dump. He included specific directions that upon arrival it was to be burned.

When he arrived back at his room that evening, however, the first thing that met his gaze was the calamander chest. Furious, he hurried down the hall to his landlady's apartment and demanded an explanation. Why had his orders been ignored?

When she was able to get a word in, the patient woman explained that the chest actually had been picked up and carted off to the dump. Upon arrival, however, the man in charge of the dump had assured the men who lugged in the chest that there must be some mistake. Nobody in his right mind, he asserted, would destroy such a beautiful and expensive article. The men must have picked up the wrong one; surely there must be another left behind, he said, which was the worthless one the owner wanted discarded.

The two men who had taken the chest to the dump, not feeling secure in their own minds about the matter, and not wishing to make a costly mistake, had returned the chest later in the day.

Completely nonplussed by this information, Maax muttered an apology to the landlady and went back to his room, where he plopped into a chair and sat staring at the chest. He would, he finally decided, give it one more chance. If nothing further happened, he would keep it; otherwise he would take immediate and drastic measures to get rid of it once and for all.

Although he had planned to attend a concert that evening, it began to rain shortly after six o'clock and he resigned himself to an evening in his room.

Before starting to read, he locked the chest with the iron key and put the key in his pocket. It was absurd that he had not thought of doing so before. This would, he felt, be the decisive test.

While he read, he maintained a keen watch on the chest, but nothing happened until well after eleven, when he put aside his book for the evening. As he closed the book and started to rise, he looked at the chest—and there was the finger.

In appearance it was unchanged. Instead of hanging slack and motionless, however, it now seemed to be imbued with faint life. It quivered slightly and it appeared to be making weak attempts to scratch the side of the chest with its long black nail.

When he finally summoned up sufficient courage, Maax took up the metal ash tray as before and crept across the room. This time he actually had the tray raised to strike before the finger vanished. It seemed to whisk back into the chest.

With a wildly thumping heart, Maax lifted the lid. Again the box was empty. But then he remembered the iron key in his pocket and a new thrill of horror coursed down his spine. The hideous digital apparition had unlocked the chest! Either that, or he was rapidly losing his sanity.

Completely unnerved, he locked the chest for a second time and then sat in a chair and watched it until two o'clock in the morning. At length, exhausted and deeply shaken, he sought his bed. Before putting out the light, he ascertained that the chest was still locked.

As soon as he fell asleep, he experienced a hideous nightmare. He dreamed that a persistent scratching sound woke him up, that he arose, lit a candle, and looked at the chest. The protruding finger showed just under the lid and this time it was galvanized with an excess of life. It twisted and turned, drummed with its thick knuckle, scratched frantically with its flat black nail. At length, as if it suddenly became aware of his presence, it became perfectly still—and then very deliberately beckoned for him to approach. Flooded with horror, he nevertheless found himself unable to disobey. Setting down the candle, he slowly crossed the room like an automaton. The monstrous beckoning finger drew him on like some infernal magnet which attracted human flesh instead of metal.

As he reached the chest, the finger darted inside and the lid immediately lifted. Overwhelmed with terror and yet utterly unable to stop himself, he stepped into the chest, sat down, drew his knees up to his chin and turned onto his side. A second later the lid slammed shut and he heard the iron key turn in the lock.

At this point in the nightmare he awoke with a ringing scream. He sat up in bed and felt the sweat of fear running down his face. In spite of the nightmare—or because of it—he dared not get up and switch on the light. Instead, he burrowed under the bedclothes and lay wide awake till morning.

After he had regained some measure of self-composure, he went out for black coffee and then, instead of reporting to his job, rode across town to the modest home of a truck driver and mover whom he had hired at various times in the past. After some quite detailed and specific plans had been agreed upon, he paid the mover ten dollars and departed with a promise to pay him an equal amount when the job was done. After lunch, considerably relieved, he went to work.

He entered his room that evening with a confident air, but as soon as he looked around, his heart sank. Contrary to instructions, the mover had not picked up the chest. It remained in the corner, just where it had been.

This time Maax was more depressed than angry. He sought out a telephone and called up the mover. The man was profusely apologetic. His truck had broken down, he explained, just as he was starting out to pick up the chest. The repairs were nearly completed, however, and he would absolutely be out to carry off the chest the first thing in the morning.

Since there was nothing else he could do, Maax thanked him and hung up. Finding himself unusually reluctant to return to his room, he ate a leisurely dinner at a nearby restaurant and later attended a movie. After the movie he stopped and had a hot chocolate. It was nearly midnight before he got back to his room.

In spite of his nightmare of the previous evening, he found himself looking forward to bed. He had lost almost an entire night's sleep and he was beginning to feel the strain.

After assuring himself that the calamander chest was securely locked, he slipped the iron key under his pillow and got into bed. In spite of his uneasiness he soon fell asleep.

Some hours later he awoke suddenly and sat up. His heart was pounding. For a moment he was not aware of what had awakened him—then he heard it. A furious scratching, tapping, thumping sound came from one corner of the room.

Trembling violently, he got out of bed, crossed the room and pressed the button on his reading lamp. Nothing happened. Either the electricity was shut off, or the light bulb had burned out.

He pulled open a drawer of the lamp stand and frantically searched for a candle. By the time he found one and applied a match to its wick the scratching sound had redoubled in intensity. The entire room seemed filled with it.

Shuddering, he lifted the candle and started across the room toward the calamander chest. As the wavering light of the candle flickered into the far corner, he saw the finger.

It protruded far out of the chest and it was writhing with furious life. It thrummed and twisted, dug at the chest with its horrible black nail, tapped and turned in an absolute frenzy of movement.

Suddenly, as he advanced, it became absolutely still. It hung down limp. Engulfed with terror, Maax was convinced that it had become aware of his approach and was now watching him.

When he was halfway across the room, the finger slowly lifted and deliberately beckoned to him. With a rush of renewed horror Maax remembered the ghastly events of his dream. Yet—as in the nightmare—he found himself utterly unable to disobey that diabolical summons. He went on like a man in a trance.

Early the next morning the mover and his assistant were let into Maax' room by the landlady. Maax had apparently already left for work, but there was no need of his presence since he had already given the mover detailed instructions in regard to the disposal of the chest.

The chest, locked but without a key, stood in one corner of the room. The melted wax remains of a candle, burned to the end of its wick, lay nearby.

The landlady shook her head. "A good way to burn the house down," she complained. "I'll have to speak to Mr. Maax. Not like him to be so careless."

The movers, burdened with the chest, paid no attention to her. The assistant growled as they started down the stairs. "Must be lined with lead. Never knew a chest so heavy before!"

"Heavy wood," his companion commented shortly, not wishing to waste his breath.

"Wonder why he's dumpin' such a good chest?" the assistant asked later as the truck approached an abandoned quarry near the edge of town.

The chief mover glanced at him slyly. "I guess I know," he said. "He bought it of Jason Kinkle. And Kinkle never told him the story on it. But he found out later, I figure—and that's why he's ditchin' it."

The assistant's interest picked up. "What's the story?" he asked.

They drove into the quarry grounds and got out of the truck.

"Kinkle bought it dirt cheap at an auction," the mover explained as they lifted out the chest. "Auction of old Henry Stubberton's furniture."

The assistant's eyes widened as they started up a steep slope with the chest. "You mean the Stubberton they found murdered in a . . ."

"In a chest!" the mover finished for him. *"This chest!"*

Neither spoke again until they set down the chest at the edge of a steep quarry shaft.

Glancing down at the deep water which filled the bottom of the shaft, the mover wiped the sweat from his face. "A pretty sight they say he was. All doubled up an turnin' black. Seems he wasn't dead when they shut him in, though. They say he must have tried to claw his way out! When they opened the chest, they found one of his fingers jammed up under the lid, near the lock! Tried to pick the lock with his fingernail, it looked like!"

The assistant shuddered. "Let's be rid of it, then. It's bad luck sure!"

The mover nodded. "Take hold and shove."

They strained together and in another second the calamander chest slipped over the edge of the quarry and hurtled toward the pool of black water far below. There was one terrific splash and then it sank from sight like a stone.

"That's good riddance and another tenner for me," the mover commented.

Oddly enough, however, he never collected the tenner, for after that day Mr. Ernest Maax dropped completely out of sight. He was never seen or heard of again. The disgruntled mover, never on the best of terms with the police, shrugged off the loss of the tenner and neglected to report the disposal of the chest. And since the landlady had never learned the mover's name, nor where he intended taking the chest, her sparse information was of no help in the search.

The police concluded that Maax had got into some scrape, changed his name, and effected a permanent change of locale.

The Poison Necklace
by MIRIAM ALLEN deFORD

The exhibit at the science fair which fascinated most
visitors was the deadly necklace fashioned by Joyce
Ledderby.

Joyce, a high school student of chemistry, had made
it of crystallized poisons. The crystals were beautiful—
green, red, yellow, orange. But within their beauty
was death; they were formed from ferrocyanides of
sodium and potassium, of copper acetate, nickel am-
monium sulfate, and dichlorate of potassium. She had

handled the poisons with extreme care, using tweezers to twist silver wire around each crystal and arrange them into the gorgeous circlet. Any one of the crystals, worn next to a living skin, would mean an agonizing death within minutes or, at the most, hours. Now they lay, mounted on black velvet, in a case under a glass lid.

And on the last day of the Science Fair someone had managed to tilt the glass unobserved and walk off with the necklace.

Joyce, coming to pick up her exhibit, found only the empty case. Dismayed and frightened, she reported her discovery to Mr. Randall, the manager of the Fair.

"A card was right by it," she stammered, "telling exactly what the crystals were made of, and warning people they were dangerous even to touch."

Mr. Randall frowned. He had not wanted to accept the exhibit in the first place, but had been persuaded by Joyce's enthusiastic chemistry teacher.

"There's only one thing to do," he decided. "We must alert the police at once. They can have announcements made on radio and television and even on movie screens, before we could possibly get a notice in any of the papers. When are you sure the necklace was last here?"

"I've come every day after school," said Joyce. "It was here at five o'clock yesterday."

"And the Fair was open last night, and all morning and afternoon till now. I've been too busy to be out on the floor at all."

Joyce burst into tears.

The lieutenant in charge of the Burglary Detail to

whom Randall was finally shunted took a long time to realize how alarming the situation was; he had never studied chemistry. When at last he got the full picture he came up with another idea: every hospital in the city, and every physician, would be alerted to watch out for a victim of the poison necklace.

It was all in vain.

Joyce Ledderby cried herself into exhaustion and was sent home in a cab. The lieutenant, now thoroughly alarmed, confessed himself stymied. "The thief must be one of three possibilities," he concluded. "An illiterate who couldn't read the card—and what would anyone like that be doing at a Science Fair? Or a complete nut—and the streets are swarming with them. Or a shrewd and cunning murderer who has protected himself and planned a perfect murder."

The Homicide Detail was called into the case. But they were as baffled as the lieutenant had been.

In the next twenty-four hours three events occurred. A woman whose bewildered husband had brought her as an anniversary present a necklace of multicolored semiprecious stones had it flung in his face by his hysterical wife, who fled the house and denounced him to the police as an attempted murderer. A hospital reported a two-year-old whose mother said he had "swallowed something"; his throat was badly burned, but X-rays revealed no necklace and his four-year-old sister finally confessed that she had fed the baby boiling soup "to see what he would do." A gang of young hoodlums knocked down an old man in a park that night and rifled his pockets; fortunately a prowl car was passing

and scattered them. They dropped their loot as they
fled, and part of it was a chain of colored stones. "My
dead wife's rosary," the old man gasped.

No other clues were developed. . . .

The person who had taken the poison necklace could
not read the card beside it; he did not go to the movies,
and would not have understood the radio and TV warn-
ings. He was a first-grader named Johnny Thayne who
had been attracted by the pretty colors and who, when
his mother's attention was elsewhere and nobody else
was looking, quickly opened the case with a grubby
handkerchief in his hand, wrapped the necklace in it,
and put the two in his pants pocket. His mother took
him away soon afterward, and by the time they got
home he had forgotten all about it.

Johnny was at school the next morning when the
doorbell rang. It was the man from Good Will Industries
for some discarded clothing Mrs. Thayne had ready for
them.

"Oh, wait a minute," she said. "I've got something
else for you. I noticed last night when I hung my little
boy's things up that the slacks he had on are almost
worn through. I'll put them in too."

In her hurry not to keep the man standing, she did
not go through the pockets.

At the Good Will plant they emptied the pockets
before putting the slacks in the washing machine. Out
came a stick of gum, two bottle caps, a good-luck penny,
and a dirty handkerchief with something in it.

Like all Good Will employees, the man in charge of

the cleaning department was handicapped. In his case his right hand had been amputated and he wore a steel-and-rubber substitute. It was with this that he drew forth the sparkling necklace.

"Look," he said to his assistant, "do you think this is something valuable, put in by mistake, that we ought to send back?"

"Phone the donor and ask," the assistant suggested. "I'll look up the name for you."

"Why no," Mrs. Thayne answered. "I haven't missed any necklace. If there was anything like that in Johnny's slacks it must be some cheap costume jewelry that he found or traded for with another kid. Just throw it away, or keep it to sell if it's worth anything."

So the chain of pretty poison crystals was given to the woman who handled the glass case full of junk jewelry.

"Oh, isn't that lovely!" she exclaimed. "I think we could charge a dollar for it. I'll put it right in the front of the case."

She reached out for it, then drew back, embarrassed. She had forgotten how sensitive Mr. Barrows was about his artificial hand; he hated to have anyone touch it. Reddening, she opened the case and looked away while he placed it carefully between a trayful of earrings and a string of dim artificial pearls.

At lunchtime two secretaries shopping around among the racks of secondhand clothing paused at the jewelry counter.

"Hey, Arlene, look at that necklace!" one of them said. "Gee, I'd like that! How much is it?"

"A dollar," the saleswoman told her.

The other girl pulled her away. "You crazy, Sandra? she demanded. "You can get as good as that any day at the five-and-ten for a dollar, and brand-new besides. You said you wanted to look at coats—well, let's look at coats."

Sandra hesitated. "Lemme try it on, anyway," she said. The saleswoman opened the case.

"Oh, come *on*," urged Arlene. "We haven't got all day."

Sandra permitted herself to be led away.

Johnny Thayne came home from school and dashed into the kitchen, where his mother was ironing.

"Hey!" he announced. "I've got a girl! She sits by me in school."

"That's nice, Johnny." Mrs. Thayne smiled. "Is she a nice girl?"

"She has red hair. Her name's Sally. Can I have a peanut butter and jelly sandwich?"

"Why not? You always do."

"Say!" said Johnny, munching. "I just remembered. I'm going to give Sally the beads I—some beads I found somewhere yesterday."

"Beads?"

"Pretty ones—all colors. They were—I picked them up at the—somewheres."

"Oh, honey, I'm so sorry!" Mrs. Thayne said. "They must have been in a pocket of your slacks that I gave to the Good Will this morning. They phoned me and I told them they weren't anything of mine and to keep them or throw them away."

Suddenly she did a double take. An item in last night's news program on TV came back to her.

"Oh, my God!" she breathed, and ran to the phone.

"Good Will? This is Mrs. Thayne. Will you connect me with whoever called me this morning about a necklace you found in my son's pocket? Hurry, please, it's urgent." Her voice shook.

She was switched from the head of the cleaning department to the saleswoman at the jewelry counter.

"That necklace? Yes, I know the one you mean. I just sold it for a dollar."

"Sold it? Oh—"

"To an old lady—for a birthday present to her granddaughter, she told me. Was it something you didn't mean us to have?"

"Listen—" No, she mustn't panic the woman; everybody at Good Will was either old or disabled, and for all she knew the clerk might drop dead of heart failure at the news. Mrs. Thayne paused to control her voice. "Do you know who she was?"

"I have no idea—just an old lady who comes in here sometimes. We call her Grandma, because she dresses so old-fashioned—all in black right down to her gloves and shoes. But I don't know her name or where she lives."

Gloves: thank heaven. And she probably wouldn't be trying the necklace on. Could the police—

The saleswoman was speaking again. "She might be here still—it was only five minutes ago."

"Will you look? It's—it's awfully important."

The clerk was a long time coming back to the phone; she was lame and couldn't walk fast.

"I'm sorry. She went out the door before I could reach her. I couldn't see which way she took."

So—the police.

But, try as they could, the police could find no trace of the old lady who had unwittingly bought death for her granddaughter.

Mrs. Kuykendahl was on old-age relief. She lived in a tiny room in a shabby rundown hotel, cooked her frugal meals surreptitiously on a hot plate, and was often hard put to find bus fare to visit her widowed daughter and the three children her daughter was bringing up by working as a chambermaid.

But Mrs. Kuykendahl had her pride; and when Bertha, her oldest grandchild and her favorite, was going to have her fourteenth birthday, her grandmother was not going to let it go unmarked. By going without some more in a life made up of going without, she had saved up a dollar for Bertha's present. The poor child never had any luxuries; this time Grandma was going to see that she had something pretty instead of practical.

When she saw that beautiful necklace, and priced at just a dollar, she knew at once that she had found what she was looking for. She was so excited that when the clerk lifted the glass cover of the case, she couldn't wait for her to bring the necklace out, but reached for it herself and held it admiringly in her mended black cotton glove.

"Yes, I'll take it," she said, and dropped it herself into the paper bag the saleswoman held out. She took the sales slip to the cashier, and having no money left to spend, paused only for a wistful glance or two at dresses and coats that would look so nice on one or another of her granddaughters before leaving the store and starting the long walk home.

She would have liked so much to wrap her gift in fancy paper and ribbons, but a dollar will stretch just so far. So she left it in the paper bag to take to Bertha's celebration, just peeping in once or twice to see how pretty it was.

The birthday was on Saturday—a day by which the police were still trying vainly to find the old lady called Grandma. Mrs. Kuykendahl had no TV or radio, and couldn't afford to buy a paper very often.

It was dark before she set out. Her daughter never got home before six, and she didn't want to arrive so early that they would feel bound to give her dinner out of their scanty stock. She got to the transfer point, and just missed the other bus. That meant a twenty-minute wait on the street corner. Oh, well. Mrs. Kuykendahl was used to patient waiting.

She leaned against the fireplug at the corner, her shabby handbag and the paper bag containing Bertha's present in one gnarled hand, the bus transfer in the other. Her feet hurt. The street lamps were few out here in this residential neighborhood, and the street was empty, unlike the downtown streets that she was used to. Occasionally an auto passed.

She sighed. She wished she were not waiting alone, and she felt relieved when she saw two teen-age boys coming down the street toward the bus stop. They were both smoking; she could see the little lights. A memory crossed the old lady's mind—herself at ten or twelve, and her mother saying to her, "Never be afraid of a man who is smoking as he walks—that means he is a respectable man who will do you no harm." She smiled; that was long before everybody smoked, women as well as men, and when it was cigars or pipes, not what they used to call coffin nails.

The two boys drew nearer.

She watched them uneasily. She didn't much like their looks after all. They were walking so fast and so softly, and it was so dark, and there was nobody else in sight.

Suddenly one was in front of her, one behind. Her arms were pinioned and her hands forced open. She started to scream, and a rough hand clamped over her lips, dislodging her upper plate so that its edge pinched the roof of her mouth.

One of the boys scooped up the handbag and the paper bag from the sidewalk, and the other—the one behind her—pushed her hard between her thin shoulder blades, so that she fell, all hundred pounds and five feet of her, on the curb. When, sick and shaking, she managed to sit up, the two teen-agers had disappeared. She tried to stand up, and her right leg buckled under her. An agonizing pain stabbed her right hip.

People finally did pass, but no one seemed to notice

her. Then a man and woman stopped at the corner to wait for the bus. "Please!" moaned old Mrs. Kuykendahl, and half an hour later she was in the Emergency Hospital.

She had given her granddaughter the best birthday present any human being can give another: she had saved her from death.

Sam Sheehan and Wallie Burnett glanced alertly all around to make sure no one was in sight but the collapsed old figure on the curb; then they walked briskly away, not running.

"Let's see what the old witch had," said Sam as they reached the safety of the deep doorway of a closed dry-cleaning shop.

He snapped open the worn handbag, gazed disparagingly at the neatly folded handkerchief, the door key, and the little tin box of aspirin tablets. He drew out the shabby purse and held it jeeringly before Wallie's eyes.

"For Pete's sake! Twenty cents!" Wallie exclaimed. "Nuts! I told you she was some old dame from the South Side, not one of the loaded broads from around here."

He laughed. Sam needed to be reminded who the leader was.

. "She didn't even have a wrist watch on her; I looked," Sam agreed gloomily. "Well, let's see what's in that paper bag you're carrying."

"Her lunch, probably." Wallie untwisted the bag and peered inside. He let out a whistle. Sam looked too.

"Well, what do you know?" he crowed. "Where'd she

get the fancy jewelry? She must've stolen it." They both chuckled.

"Come on," Wallie ordered. "We'll go over to your place. Your old lady'll be out."

"Half of it's mine," said Sam defensively.

"OK, OK. What we've got to do is sell it and split the money."

"Do you think it's real?"

"How would I know? It don't look like cheap junk, that's all I know. Let's get a look at it in a good light. If it's worth anything, I know where we can get the best price for it."

"Where?"

"That's telling." Wallie said derisively. "Who's running this business, anyway?"

"All right, Wallie." Sam's tone was placating, as befitted the younger and smaller member of the firm. "But mightn't we get more if somebody offered a reward for it?"

"Who? That old bat with twenty cents on her? Be your age."

Sam was silent, as became a neophyte. Wallie would stop taking him along on these muggings and heists if he didn't keep his mouth buttoned more.

They went up in the housing-project elevator to Sam's apartment, Wallie holding the paper bag under his jacket in case they met anybody. Sam's mother worked at night, cleaning in an office building downtown.

Sam locked the door behind them, switched on the light, and pulled down the shades. When he turned around, Wallie had taken the necklace from the bag and was holding it by either end under the ceiling light, gazing at it appraisingly.

"I'll bet you a thousand dollars this stuff is real," he said. "Look how the stones shine."

"Lemme see." Sam reached out for it.

"Wait a minute." Wallie jerked it back. "You'll get your turn."

Sam, emboldened, grabbed it and pulled. The delicate silver wire with which Joyce Ledderby had fashioned the necklace gave way, and the crystals fell in a rainbow heap on the linoleum-covered floor.

"Now look what you done!" Wallie aimed a swipe at Sam that stung. Both boys got down on their knees and began to pick up the shining crystals and put them back into the crumpled paper bag. Sam's left eye hurt where Wallie had hit him; he freed one hand to rub the place hard. Wallie blew a wet razzberry at him that scattered spittle; he wiped his mouth with grimy fingers that were still holding one of the pretty stones.

"Boy!" he said. "This stuff is *real*. It'll set us up for life!"

Sam nodded his agreement.

"It'll do that all right," he echoed. "It's the living end!"

The Bottle Imp
by ROBERT LOUIS STEVENSON

There was a man of the island of Hawaii, whom I shall
call Keawe; for the truth is, he still lives, and his name
must be kept secret; but the place of his birth was not
far from Honaunau, where the bones of Keawe the
Great lie hidden in a cave. This man was poor, brave,
and active; he could read and write like a schoolmaster;
he was a first-rate mariner besides, sailed for some time
in the island steamers, and steered a whaleboat on the
Kamakua coast. At length it came in Keawe's mind to

have a sight of the great world and foreign cities, and he shipped on a vessel bound to San Francisco.

This is a fine town, with a fine harbor, and rich people uncountable; and, in particular, there is one hill which is covered with palaces. Upon this hill Keawe was one day taking a walk, with his pocket full of money, viewing the great houses upon either hand with pleasure. "What fine houses there are!" he was thinking. "And how happy must these people be who dwell in them, and take no care for the morrow!" The thought was in his mind when he came abreast of a house that was smaller than some others, but all finished and beautified like a toy; the steps of that house shone like silver, and the borders of the garden bloomed like garlands, and the windows were bright like diamonds; and Keawe stopped and wondered at the excellence of all he saw. So stopping, he was aware of a man who looked forth upon him through a window, so clear that Keawe could see him as you see a fish in a pool upon the reef. The man was elderly, with a bald head and a black beard; and his face was heavy with sorrow, and he bitterly sighed. And the truth of it is, that as Keawe looked in upon the man, and the man looked out upon Keawe, each envied the other.

All of a sudden the man smiled and nodded, and beckoned Keawe to enter, and met him at the door of the house.

"This is a fine house of mine," said the man, and bitterly sighed. "Would you not care to view the chambers?"

So he led Keawe all over it, from the cellar to the

roof, and there was nothing there that was not perfect of its kind, and Keawe was astonished.

"Truly," said Keawe, "this is a beautiful house; if I lived in the like of it, I should be laughing all day long. How comes it, then, that you should be sighing?"

"There is no reason," said the man, "why you should not have a house in all points similar to this, and finer, if you wish. You have some money, I suppose?"

"I have fifty dollars," said Keawe; "but a house like this will cost more than fifty dollars."

The man made a computation. "I am sorry you have no more," said he, "for it may raise you trouble in the future; but it shall be yours at fifty dollars."

"The house?" asked Keawe.

"No, not the house," replied the man; "but the bottle. For I must tell you, although I appear to you so rich and fortunate, all my fortune, and this house itself and its garden, came out of a bottle not much bigger than a pint. This is it."

And he opened a lockfast place, and took out a round-bellied bottle with a long neck; the glass of it was white like milk, with changing rainbow colors in the grain. Withinsides something obscurely moved, like a shadow and a fire.

"This is the bottle," said the man. And when Keawe laughed, "You do not believe me?" he added. "Try, then, for yourself. See if you can break it."

So Keawe took the bottle up and dashed it on the floor till he was weary; but it jumped on the floor like a child's ball, and was not injured.

"This is a strange thing," said Keawe. "For by the

touch of it, as well as by the look, the bottle should be of glass."

"Of glass it is," replied the man, sighing more heavily than ever; "but the glass of it was tempered in the flames of hell. An imp lives in it, and that is the shadow we behold there moving; or, so I suppose. If any man buy this bottle the imp is at his command; all that he desires—love, fame, money, houses like this house, ay, or a city like this city—all are his at the word uttered. Napoleon had this bottle, and by it he grew to be the king of the world; but he sold it at the last and fell. Captain Cook had this bottle, and by it he found his way to so many islands; but he too sold it, and was slain upon Hawaii. For, once it is sold, the power goes and the protection; and unless a man remain content with what he has, ill will befall him."

"And yet you talk of selling it yourself?" Keawe said.

"I have all I wish, and I am growing elderly," replied the man. "There is one thing the imp cannot do—he cannot prolong life; and it would not be fair to conceal from you there is a drawback to the bottle; for if a man die before he sells it, he must burn in hell forever."

"To be sure, that is a drawback and no mistake," cried Keawe. "I would not meddle with the thing. I can do without a house, thank God; but there is one thing I could not be doing with one particle, and that is to be damned."

"Dear me, you must not run away with things," returned the man. "All you have to do is to use the power of the imp in moderation, and then sell it to someone else, as I do to you, and finish your life in comfort."

"Well, I observe two things," said Keawe. "All the time you keep sighing like a maid in love—that is one; and for the other, you sell this bottle very cheap."

"I have told you already why I sigh," said the man. "It is because I fear my health is breaking up; and, as you said yourself, to die and go to the devil is a pity for anyone. As for why I sell so cheap, I must explain to you there is a peculiarity about the bottle. Long ago, when the devil brought it first upon earth, it was extremely expensive, and was sold first of all to Prester John for many millions of dollars; but it cannot be sold at all, unless sold at a loss. If you sell it for as much as you paid for it, back it comes to you again like a homing pigeon. It follows that the price has kept falling in these centuries, and the bottle is now remarkably cheap. I bought it myself from one of my great neighbors on this hill, and the price I paid was only ninety dollars. I could sell it for as high as eighty-nine dollars and ninety-nine cents, but not a penny dearer, or back the thing must come to me. Now, about this there are two bothers. First, when you offer a bottle so singular for eighty-odd dollars, people suppose you to be jesting. And second—but there is no hurry about that—and I need not go into it. Only remember it must be coined money that you sell it for."

"How am I to know that this is all true?" asked Keawe.

"Some of it you can try at once," replied the man. "Give me your fifty dollars, take the bottle, and wish your fifty dollars back into your pocket. If that does not happen, I pledge you my honor I will cry off the bargain and restore your money."

"You are not deceiving me?" said Keawe.

The man bound himself with a great oath.

"Well, I will risk that much," said Keawe, "for that can do no harm," and he paid over his money to the man, and the man handed him the bottle.

"Imp of the bottle," said Keawe, "I want my fifty dollars back." And sure enough, he had scarce said the word before his pocket was as heavy as ever.

"To be sure this is a wonderful bottle," said Keawe.

"And now good-morning to you, my fine fellow, and the devil go with you for me," said the man.

"Hold on," said Keawe. "I don't want any more of this fun. Here, take your bottle back."

"You have bought it for less than I paid for it," replied the man, rubbing his hands. "It is yours now; and, for my part, I am only concerned to see the back of you." And with that he rang for his Chinese servant, and had Keawe shown out of the house.

Now, when Keawe was in the street, with the bottle under his arm, he began to think. "If all is true about this bottle, I may have made a losing bargain," thinks he. "But perhaps the man was only fooling me." The first thing he did was to count his money; the sum was exact—forty-nine dollars American money, and one Chili piece. "That looks like the truth," said Keawe. "Now I will try another part."

The streets in that part of the city were as clean as a ship's decks, and though it was noon, there were no passengers. Keawe set the bottle in the gutter and walked away. Twice he looked back, and there was the milky, round-bellied bottle where he left it. A third time he looked back and turned a corner; but he had scarce done so, when something knocked upon his elbow, and behold! it was the long neck sticking up; and as for the round belly, it was jammed into the pocket of his pilot-coat.

"And that looks like the truth," said Keawe.

The next thing he did was to buy a corkscrew in a shop, and go apart in a secret place in the fields. And there he tried to draw the cork, but as often as he put the screw in, out it came again, and the cork was as whole as ever.

"There is some new sort of cork," said Keawe, and all at once he began to shake and sweat, for he was afraid of that bottle.

On his way back to the port-side he saw a shop where a man sold shells and clubs from the wild islands, old heathen deities, old coined money, pictures from China and Japan, and all manner of things that sailors bring in their sea-chests. And here he had an idea. So he went in and offered the bottle for a hundred dollars. The man of the shop laughed at him at first and offered him five; but, indeed, it was a curious bottle, such glass was never blown in any human glass-works, so prettily the colors shone under the milky way, and so strangely the shadow hovered in the midst; so, after he had disputed a while after the manner of his kind, the shopman gave Keawe sixty silver dollars for the thing and set it on a shelf in the midst of his window.

"Now," said Keawe, "I have sold that for sixty which I bought for fifty—or, to say truth, a little less, because one of my dollars was from Chili. Now I shall know the truth upon another point."

So he went back on board his ship, and when he opened his chest, there was the bottle, which had come more quickly than himself. Now Keawe had a mate on board whose name was Lopaka.

"What ails you," said Lopaka, "that you stare in your chest?"

They were alone in the ship's forecastle, and Keawe bound him to secrecy, and told all.

"This is a very strange affair," said Lopaka; "and I fear you will be in trouble about this bottle. But there is one point very clear—that you are sure of the trouble, and you had better have the profit in the bargain. Make up your mind what you want with it, give the order, and when it is done as you desire, I will buy the bottle myself; for I have an idea of my own to get a schooner, and go trading through the islands."

"That is not my idea," said Keawe; "but to have a beautiful house and garden on the Kona coast, where I was born, the sun shining in at the door, flowers in the garden, glass in the windows, pictures on the walls, and toys and fine carpets on the tables, for all the world like the house I was in this day—only a story higher, and with balconies all about like the King's palace; and to live there without care and make merry with my friends and relatives."

"Well," said Lopaka, "let us carry it back with us to Hawaii; and if all comes true as you suppose, I will buy the bottle, as I said, and ask for a schooner."

Upon that they were agreed, and it was not long

before the ship returned to Honolulu, carrying Keawe and Lopaka, and the bottle. They were scarce come ashore when they met a friend upon the beach, who began at once to condole with Keawe.

"I do not know what I am to be condoled about," said Keawe.

"Is it possible you have not heard," said the friend, "your uncle—that good old man—is dead, and your cousin—that beautiful boy—was drowned at sea?"

Keawe was filled with sorrow, and beginning to weep and to lament, he forgot about the bottle. But Lopaka was thinking to himself, and presently, when Keawe's grief was a little abated, "I have been thinking," said Lopaka. "Had not your uncle lands in Hawaii, in the district of Kaü?"

"No," said Keawe, "not in Kaü: they are on the mountain side—a little south of Hookena."

"These lands will now be yours?" asked Lopaka.

"And so they will," says Keawe, and began again to lament for his relatives.

"No," said Lopaka, "do not lament at present. I have a thought in my mind. How if this should be the doing of the bottle? For here is the place ready for your house."

"If this be so," cried Keawe, "it is a very ill way to serve me by killing my relatives. But it may be, indeed; for it was in just such a station that I saw the house with my mind's eye."

"The house, however, is not yet built," said Lopaka.

"No, nor like to be!" said Keawe. "For though my uncle has some coffee and ava and bananas, it will not be more than will keep me in comfort; and the rest of that land is the black lava."

"Let us go to the lawyer," said Lopaka; "I have still this idea in my mind."

Now, when they came to the lawyer's, it appeared Keawe's uncle had grown monstrous rich in the last days, and there was a fund of money.

"And here is the money for the house!" cried Lopaka.

"If you are thinking of a new house," said the lawyer, "here is the card of a new architect of whom they tell me great things."

"Better and better!" cried Lopaka. "Here is all made plain for us. Let us continue to obey orders."

So they went to the architect, and he had drawings of houses on his table.

"You want something out of the way," said the architect. "How do you like this?" and he handed a drawing to Keawe.

Now, when Keawe set eyes on the drawing, he cried out aloud, for it was the picture of his thought exactly drawn.

"I am in for this house," thought he. "Little as I like the way it comes to me, I am in for it now, and I may as well take the good along with the evil."

So he told the architect all that he wished, and how he would have that house furnished, and about the pictures on the wall and the knickknacks on the tables; and he asked the man plainly for how much he would undertake the whole affair.

The architect put many questions, and took his pen and made a computation; and when he had done he named the very sum that Keawe had inherited.

Lopaka and Keawe looked at one another and nodded.

"It is quite clear," thought Keawe, "that I am to have this house, whether or no. It comes from the devil, and I fear I will get little good by that; and of one thing I am sure, I will make no more wishes as long as I have this bottle. But with the house I am saddled, and I may as well take the good along with the evil."

So he made his terms with the architect, and they signed a paper; and Keawe and Lopaka took ship again and sailed to Australia; for it was concluded between them they should not interfere at all, but leave the architect and the bottle imp to build and to adorn the house at their own pleasure.

The voyage was a good voyage, only all the time Keawe was holding in his breath, for he had sworn he would utter no more wishes, and take no more favors, from the devil. The time was up when they got back. The architect told them that the house was ready, and Keawe and Lopaka took passage in the *Hall,* and went down Kona way to view the house, and see if all had been done fitly according to the thought that was in Keawe's mind.

Now, the house stood on the mountainside, visible to ships. Above, the forest ran up into the clouds of rain; below, the black lava fell in cliffs, where the kings of old lay buried. A garden bloomed about the house with every hue of flowers; and there was an orchard of papaia on the one hand and an orchard of breadfruit on the other, and right in front, towards the sea, a ship's mast had been rigged up and bore a flag. As for the house, it was three stories high, with great chambers and broad balconies on each. The windows were of glass, so excellent that it was as clear as water and as bright as day. All manner of furniture adorned the chambers. Pictures hung upon the wall in golden frames—pictures of ships, and men fighting, and of the most beautiful women, and of singular places; nowhere in the world are there pictures of so bright a color as those Keawe found hanging in his house. As for the knickknacks, they were extraordinarily fine: chiming clocks and musical boxes, little men with nodding heads, books filled with pictures, weapons of price from all quarters of the world, and the most elegant puzzles to entertain the leisure of a solitary man. And as no one would care to live in such chambers only to walk through and view them, the balconies were made so broad that a whole town might have lived upon them in delight; and Keawe knew not which to prefer, whether the back porch, where you get the land breeze and looked upon the orchards and the flowers, or the front balcony, where you could drink the wind of the sea, and look down the steep wall of the mountain and see the *Hall* going by once a week or so between Hookena and the hills of Pele, or the schooners plying up the coast for food and ava and bananas.

When they had viewed all, Keawe and Lopaka sat on the porch.

"Well," asked Lopaka, "is it all as you designed?"

"Words cannot utter it," said Keawe. "It is better than I dreamed, and I am sick with satisfaction."

"There is but one thing to consider," said Lopaka.
"All this may be quite natural, and the bottle imp have nothing whatever to say to it. If I were to buy the bottle, and got no schooner after all, I should have put my hand in the fire for nothing. I gave you my word, I know; but yet I think you would not grudge me one more proof."

"I have sworn I would take no more favors," said Keawe. "I have gone already deep enough."

"This is no favor I am thinking of," replied Lopaka. "It is only to see the imp himself. There is nothing to be gained by that, and so nothing to be ashamed of, and yet, if I once saw him, I should be sure of the whole matter. So indulge me so far, and let me see the imp; and, after that, here is the money in my hand; and I will buy it."

"There is only one thing I am afraid of," said Keawe. "The imp may be very ugly to view, and if you once set eyes upon him you might be very undesirous of the bottle."

"I am a man of my word," said Lopaka. "And here is the money betwixt us."

"Very well," replied Keawe, "I have a curiosity myself. So come, let us have one look at you, Mr. Imp."

Now as soon as that was said, the imp looked out of the bottle, and in again, swift as a lizard; and there sat Keawe and Lopaka turned to stone. The night had quite come before either found a thought to say or voice to say it with; and then Lopaka pushed the money over and took the bottle.

"I am a man of my word," said he, "and had need to

be so, or I would not touch this bottle with my foot. Well, I shall get my schooner and a dollar or two for my pocket; and then I will be rid of this devil as fast as I can. For, to tell you the plain truth, the look of him has cast me down."

"Lopaka," said Keawe, "do not you think any worse of me than you can help; I know it is night, and the roads bad, and the pass by the tombs an ill place to go by so late, but I declare since I have seen that little face, I cannot eat or sleep or pray till it is gone from me. I will give you a lantern, and a basket to put the bottle in, and any picture or fine thing in all my house that takes your fancy; and be gone at once, and go sleep at Hookena with Nahinu."

"Keawe," said Lopaka, "many a man would take this ill; above all, when I am doing you a turn so friendly as to keep my word and buy the bottle; and for that matter, the night and the dark, and the way by the tombs, must be all tenfold more dangerous to a man with such a sin upon his conscience and such a bottle under his arm. But for my part, I am so extremely terrified myself, I have not the heart to blame you. Here I go, then; and I pray God you may be happy in your house, and I fortunate with my schooner, and both get to heaven in the end in spite of the devil and his bottle."

So Lopaka went down the mountain; and Keawe stood in his front balcony, and listened to the clink of the horses' shoes, and watched the lantern go shining down the path, and along the cliff of caves where the old dead are buried; and all the time he trembled and clasped his hands, and prayed for his friend, and gave glory to God that he himself was escaped out of that trouble.

But the next day came very brightly, and that new house of his was so delightful to behold that he forgot his terrors. One day followed another, and Keawe dwelt there in perpetual joy. He had his place on the back porch; it was there he ate and lived, and read the stories in the Honolulu newspapers; but when anyone came by they would go in and view the chambers and the pictures. And the fame of the house went far and wide; it was called *Ka-Hale Nui*—the Great House— in all Kona; and sometimes the Bright House, for Keawe kept a Chinese, who was all day dusting and furbishing; and the glass, and the gilt, and the fine stuffs, and the pictures, shone as bright as the morning. As for Keawe himself, he could not walk in the chambers without singing, his heart was so enlarged; and when ships sailed by upon the sea, he would fly his colors on the mast.

So time went by, until one day Keawe went upon a visit as far as Kailua to certain of his friends. There he was well feasted, and left as soon as he could the next morning, and rode hard, for he was impatient to behold his beautiful house; and, besides, the night then coming on was the night in which the dead of old days go abroad in the sides of Kona; and having already meddled with the devil, he was the more chary of meeting with the dead. A little beyond Honaunau, looking far ahead, he was aware of a woman bathing in the edges of the sea; and she seemed a well-grown girl, but he thought no more of it. Then he saw her white shift flutter as she put it on, and then her red holoku; and by the time he came abreast of her she was done with her toilet, and had come up from the sea, and stood by the trackside in her red holoku, and she was all freshened with the bath, and her eyes shone and were kind. Now Keawe no sooner beheld her than he drew rein.

"I thought I knew everyone in this country," said he. "How comes it that I do not know you?"

"I am Kokua, daughter of Kiano," said the girl, "and I have just returned from Oahu. Who are you?"

"I will tell you who I am in a little," said Keawe, dismounting from his horse, "but not now. For I have a thought in my mind, and if you knew who I was, you might have heard of me, and would not give me a true answer. But tell me, first of all, one thing: are you married?"

At this Kokua laughed out aloud. "It is you who ask questions," she said. "Are you married yourself?"

"Indeed, Kokua, I am not," replied Keawe, "and never thought to be until this hour. But here is the plain truth. I have met you here at the roadside, and I saw your eyes, which are like the stars, and my heart went to you as swift as a bird. And so now, if you want none of me, say so, and I will go on to my own place; but if you think me no worse than any other young man, say so, too, and I will turn aside to your father's for the night, and tomorrow I will talk with the good man."

Kokua said never a word, but she looked at the sea and laughed.

"Kokua," said Keawe, "if you say nothing, I will take that for the good answer; so let us be stepping to your father's door."

She went on ahead of him, still without speech; only sometimes she glanced back and glanced away again, and she kept the strings of her hat in her mouth.

Now, when they had come to the door, Kiano came out on his veranda, and cried out and welcomed Keawe by name. At that the girl looked over, for the fame of the great house had come to her ears; and, to be sure, it was a great temptation. All that evening they were very merry together; and the girl was as bold as brass under the eyes of her parents, and made a mark of Keawe, for she had a quick wit. The next day he had a word with Kiano, and found the girl alone.

"Kokua," said he, "you made a mark of me all the evening; and it is still time to bid me go. I would not tell you who I was, because I have so fine a house, and I feared you would think too much of that house and too little of the man who loves you. Now you know all, and if you wish to have seen the last of me, say so at once."

"No," said Kokua, but this time she did not laugh, nor did Keawe ask for more.

This was the wooing of Keawe; things had gone quickly; but so an arrow goes, and the ball of a rifle swifter still, and yet both may strike the target. Things had gone fast, but they had gone far also, and the thought of Keawe rang in the maiden's head; she heard his voice in the breach of the surf upon the lava, and for this young man whom she had seen but twice she would have left father and mother and her native islands. As for Keawe himself, his horse flew up the path of the mountain under the cliff of tombs, and the sound of the hoofs, and the sound of Keawe singing to himself for pleasure, echoed in the caverns of the dead. He came to the Bright House, and still he was singing. He sat and ate in the broad balcony, and the Chinese wondered at his master, to hear how he sang between the mouthfuls. The sun went down into the sea, and the night came; and Keawe walked the balconies by lamplight, high on the mountains, and the voice of his singing startled men on ships.

"Here am I now upon my high place," he said to himself. "Life may be no better; this is the mountaintop. For the first time I will light up the chambers, and bathe in my fine bath with the hot water and the cold, and sleep above in the bed of my bridal chamber."

So the Chinese had word, and he must rise from sleep and light the furnaces; and as he walked below, beside the boilers, he heard his master singing and rejoicing above him in the lighted chambers. When the water began to be hot the Chinese cried to his master: and Keawe went into the bathroom; and the Chinese heard him sing as he filled the marble basin; and heard him sing, and the singing broken, as he undressed; until of a sudden, the song ceased. The Chinese listened, and listened; he called up to ask if all were well, and Keawe answered him "Yes," and bade him go to bed; but there was no more singing in the Bright House; and all night long the Chinese heard his master's feet go round and round the balconies without repose.

Now, the truth of it was this: as Keawe undressed for his bath, he spied upon his flesh a patch like a patch of lichen on a rock, and it was then that he stopped singing. For he knew the likeness of that patch, and knew that he was fallen in the Chinese Evil.*

Now, it is a sad thing for any man to fall into this sickness. And it would be a sad thing for anyone to leave a house so beautiful and so commodious, and depart from all his friends to the north coast of Molokai, between the mighty cliff and the sea breakers. But what was that to the case of the man Keawe, he who had met his love but yesterday and won her but that morning, and now saw all his hopes break, in a moment, like a piece of glass?

A while he sat upon the edge of the bath, then sprang, with a cry, and ran outside; and to and fro, to and fro, along the balcony, like one despairing.

"Very willingly could I leave Hawaii, the home of my fathers," Keawe was thinking. "Very lightly could I leave my house, the high-placed, the many-windowed, here upon the mountains. Very bravely could I go to Molokai, to Kalaupapa by the cliffs, to live with the smitten and to sleep there, far from my fathers. But what wrong have I done, what sin lies upon my soul, that I should have encountered Kokua coming cool from the sea water in the evening? Kokua, the soul ensnarer! Kokua, the light of my life! Her may I never wed, her may I look upon no longer, her may I no more handle with my loving hand; and it for this, it is for you, O Kokua! that I pour my lamentations!"

Now you are to observe what sort of a man Keawe was, for he might have dwelt there in the Bright House for years, and no one been the wiser of his sickness; but

* Leprosy.

he reckoned nothing of that, if he must lose Kokua. And again he might have wed Kokua even as he was; and so many would have done, because they have the souls of pigs; but Keawe loved the maid manfully, and he would do her no hurt and bring her in no danger.

A little beyond the midst of the night, there came in his mind the recollection of that bottle. He went round to the back porch, and called to memory the day when the devil had looked forth; and at the thought ice ran in his veins.

"A dreadful thing is in the bottle," thought Keawe, "and dreadful is the imp, and it is a dreadful thing to risk the flames of hell. But what other hope have I to cure my sickness or to wed Kokua? What!" he thought. "Would I beard the devil once, only to get me a house, and not face him again to win Kokua?"

Thereupon he called to mind it was the next day the *Hall* went by on her return to Honolulu. "There must I go first," he thought, "and see Lopaka. For the best hope that I have now is to find that same bottle I was so pleased to be rid of."

Never a wink could he sleep; the food stuck in his throat; but he sent a letter to Kiano and, about the time when the steamer would be coming, rode down beside the cliff of the tombs. It rained; his horse went heavily; he looked up at the black mouths of the caves, and he envied the dead that slept there and were done with trouble; and called to mind how he had galloped by the day before, and was astonished. So he came down to Hookena, and there was all the country gathered for the steamer as usual. In the shed before the store they sat and jested and passed the news; but there was no matter of speech in Keawe's bosom, and he sat in their midst and looked out on the rain falling on the houses, and the surf beating among the rocks, and the sighs arose in his throat.

"Keawe of the Bright House is out of spirits," said one to another. Indeed, and so he was, and little wonder.

Then the *Hall* came, and the whaleboat carried him on board. The afterpart of the ship was full of Haoles*—who had been to visit the volcano, as their custom is; and the midst was crowded with Kanakas, and the forepart with wild bulls from Hilo and horses from Kaü; but Keawe sat apart from all in his sorrow, and watched for the house of Kiano. There it sat low upon the shore in the black rocks, and shaded by the cocoa palms, and there by the door was a red holoku, no greater than a fly, and going to and fro with a fly's busyness. "Ah, queen of my heart," he cried, "I'll venture my dear soul to win you!"

Soon after, darkness fell and the cabins were lit up, and the Haoles sat and played at the cards and drank whisky as their custom is; but Keawe walked the deck all night; and all the next day, as they steamed under the lee of Maui or of Molokai, he was still pacing to and fro like a wild animal in a menagerie.

Towards evening they passed Diamond Head, and came to the pier of Honolulu. Keawe stepped out among the crowd and began to ask for Lopaka. It seemed he had become the owner of a schooner—none better in the islands— and was gone upon an adventure as far as

* Whites.

Pola-Pola or Kahiki; so there was no help to be looked for from Lopaka. Keawe called to mind a friend of his, a lawyer in the town, (I must not tell his name), and inquired of him. They said he was grown suddenly rich, and had a fine new house upon Waikiki shore; and this put a thought in Keawe's head, and he called a hack and drove to the lawyer's house.

The house was all brand-new, and the trees in the garden no greater than walking sticks, and the lawyer, when he came, had the air of a man well pleased.

"What can I do to serve you?" said the lawyer.

"You are a friend of Lopaka's," replied Keawe, "and Lopaka purchased from me a certain piece of goods that I thought you might enable me to trace."

The lawyer's face became very dark. "I do not profess to misunderstand you, Mr. Keawe," said he, "though this is an ugly business to be stirring in. You may be sure I know nothing, but yet I have a guess, and if you would apply in a certain quarter I think you might have news."

And he named the name of a man, which, again, I had better not repeat. So it was for days, and Keawe went from one to another, finding everywhere new clothes and carriages, and fine new houses, and men everywhere in great contentment, although, to be sure, when he hinted at his business their faces would cloud over.

"No doubt I am upon the track," thought Keawe. "These new clothes and carriages are all the gifts of the little imp, and these glad faces are the faces of men who have taken their profit and got rid of the accursed thing in safety. When I see pale cheeks and hear sighing,

I shall know that I am near the bottle."

So it befell at last he was recommended to a Haole in Beritania Street. When he came to the door, about the hour of the evening meal, there were the usual marks of the new house, and the young garden, and the electric light shining in the windows; but when the owner came, a shock of hope and fear ran through Keawe; for here was a young man, white as a corpse, and black about the eyes, the hair shedding from his head, and such a look in his countenance as a man may have when he is waiting for the gallows.

"Here it is, to be sure," thought Keawe, and so with this man he noways veiled his errand. "I am come to buy the bottle," said he.

At the word, the young Haole of Beritania Street reeled against the wall.

"The bottle!" he gasped. "To buy the bottle!" Then he seemed to choke, and seizing Keawe by the arm, carried him into a room and poured out wine in two glasses.

"Here is my respects," said Keawe, who had been much about with Haoles in his time. "Yes," he added, "I am come to buy the bottle. What is the price by now?"

At that word the young man let his glass slip through his fingers, and looked upon Keawe like a ghost.

"The price," says he; "the price! You do not know the price?"

"It is for that I am asking you," returned Keawe. "But why are you so much concerned? Is there anything wrong about the price?"

"It has dropped a great deal in value since your time,

Mr. Keawe," said the young man, stammering.

"Well, well, I shall have the less to pay for it," said Keawe. "How much did it cost you?"

The young man was as white as a sheet.

"Two cents," said he.

"What!" cried Keawe. "Two cents? Why, then, you can only sell it for one. And he who buys it——" The words died upon Keawe's tongue; he who bought it could never sell it again, the bottle and the bottle imp must abide with him until he died, and when he died must carry him to the red end of hell.

The young man of Beritania Street fell upon his knees. "For God's sake, buy it!" he cried. "You can have all my fortune in the bargain. I was mad when I bought it at that price. I had embezzled money at my store; I was lost else; I must have gone to jail."

"Poor creature," said Keawe, "you would risk your soul upon so desperate an adventure, and to avoid the proper punishment of your own disgrace; and you think I could hesitate with love in front of me. Give me the bottle, and the change which I am sure you have all ready. Here is a five-cent piece."

It was as Keawe supposed; the young man had the change ready in a drawer; the bottle changed hands, and Keawe's fingers were no sooner clasped upon the stalk than he had breathed his wish to be a clean man. And sure enough, when he got home to his room, and stripped himself before a glass, his flesh was whole like an infant's. And here was the strange thing: he had no sooner seen this miracle than his mind was changed within him, and he cared naught for the Chinese Evil, and little enough for Kokua; and had but the one thought, that here he was bound to the bottle imp for time and for eternity, and had no better hope but to be a cinder forever in the flames of hell. Away ahead of him he saw them blaze with his mind's eye, and his soul shrank, and darkness fell upon the light.

When Keawe came to himself a little, he was aware it was the night when the band played at the hotel. Thither he went, because he feared to be alone; and there, among happy faces, walked to and fro, and heard the tunes go up and down, and all the while he heard the flames crackle and saw the red fire burning in the bottomless pit. Of a sudden the band played *Hiki-ao-ao;* that was a song that he had sung with Kokua, and at the strain courage returned to him.

"It is done now," he thought, "and once more let me take the good along with the evil."

So it befell that he returned to Hawaii by the first steamer, and as soon as it could be managed he was wedded to Kokua, and carried her up the mountainside to the Bright House.

Now it was so with these two, that when they were together Keawe's heart was stilled; but as soon as he was alone he fell into a brooding horror, and heard the flames crackle, and saw the red fire burn in the bottomless pit. The girl, indeed, had come to him wholly; her heart leaped in her side at sight of him, her hand clung to his; and she was so fashioned, from the hair upon her head to the nails upon her toes, that none could see her without joy. She was pleasant in her nature. She had the good word always. Full of song she was, and went to and fro in the Bright House, the brightest thing in its three stories, carolling like the birds. And Keawe beheld and heard her with delight, and then must shrink upon one side, and weep and groan to think upon the price that he had paid for her; and then he must dry his eyes, and wash his face, and go and sit with her on the broad balconies, joining in her songs, and, with a sick spirit, answering her smiles.

There came a day when her feet began to be heavy and her songs more rare; and now it was not Keawe only that would weep apart, but each would sunder from the other and sit in opposite balconies with the whole width of the Bright House betwixt. Keawe was so sunk in his despair, he scarce observed the change, and was only glad he had more hours to sit alone and brood upon his destiny, and was not so frequently condemned to pull a smiling face on a sick heart. But one day, coming softly through the house, he heard the sound of a child sobbing, and there was Kokua rolling her face upon the balcony floor, and weeping like the lost.

"You do well to weep in this house, Kokua," he said. "And yet I would give the head off my body that you (at least) might have been happy."

"Happy!" she cried. "Keawe, when you lived alone in your Bright House you were the word of the island for a happy man; laughter and song were in your mouth, and your face was as bright as the sunrise. Then you wedded poor Kokua; and the good God knows what is amiss in her—but from that day you have not smiled. Oh!" she cried. "What ails me? I thought I was pretty, and I knew I loved him. What ails me, that I throw this cloud upon my husband?"

"Poor Kokua," said Keawe. He sat down by her side, and sought to take her hand; but that she plucked away. "Poor Kokua," he said again. "My poor child—my pretty. And I had thought all this while to spare you! Well, you shall know all. Then, at least, you will pity poor Keawe; then you will understand how much he loved you in the past— that he dared hell for your possession—and how much he loves you still (the poor condemned one), that he can yet call up a smile when he beholds you."

With that he told her all, even from the beginning.

"You have done this for me?" she cried. "Ah, well, then what do I care!" and she wept upon him.

"Ah, child!" said Keawe. "And yet, when I consider the fire of hell, I care a good deal!"

"Never tell me," said she, "no man can be lost because he loved Kokua, and no other fault. I tell you, Keawe, I shall save you with these hands, or perish in your company. What! You loved me and gave your soul, and you think I will not die to save you in return?"

"Ah, my dear, you might die a hundred times: and what difference would that make," he cried, "except to leave me lonely till the time comes for my damnation?"

"You know nothing," said she. "I was educated in a school in Honolulu; I am no common girl. And I tell you I shall save my lover. What is this you say about a cent? But all the world is not American. In England they have a piece they call a farthing, which is about half a cent.

Ah! sorrow!" she cried. "That makes it scarcely better, for the buyer must be lost, and we shall find none so brave as my Keawe! But, then, there is France; they have a small coin there which they call a centime, and these go five to the cent, or thereabout. We could not do better. Come, Keawe, let us go to the French islands; let us go to Tahiti as fast as ships can bear us. There we have four centimes, three centimes, two centimes, one centime; four possible sales to come and go on; and two of us to push the bargain. Come, my Keawe! Kiss me, and banish care. Kokua will defend you."

"Gift of God!" he cried. "I cannot think that God will punish me for desiring aught so good. Be it as you will then, take me where you please: I put my life and my salvation in your hands."

Early the next day Kokua went about her preparations. She took Keawe's chest that he used when sailoring; and first she put the bottle in a corner, and then packed it with the richest of their clothes and the bravest of the knickknacks in the house. "For," said she, "we must seem to be rich folks, or who would believe in the bottle?" All the time of her preparation she was as gay as a bird; only when she looked upon Keawe the tears would spring in her eye, and she must run and kiss him. As for Keawe, a weight was off his soul; now that he had his secret shared, and some hope in front of him, he seemed like a new man, his feet went lightly on the earth, and his breath was good to him again. Yet was terror still at his elbow; and ever and again, as the wind blows out a taper, hope died in him, and he saw the flames toss and the red fire burn in hell.

It was given out in the country they were gone pleasuring in the States, which was thought a strange thing, and yet not so strange as the truth, if any could have guessed it. So they went to Honolulu in the *Hall,* and thence in the *Umatilla* to San Francisco with a crowd of Haoles, and at San Francisco took their passage by the mail brigantine, the *Tropic Bird,* for Papeete, the chief place of the French in the south islands. Thither they came, after a pleasant voyage, on a fair day of the Trade Wind, and saw the reef with the surf breaking and Motuiti with its palms, and the white houses of the town low down along the shore among green trees, and overhead the mountains and the clouds of Tahiti, the wise island.

It was judged the most wise to hire a house, which they did accordingly, opposite the British Consul's, to make a great parade of money, and themselves conspicuous with carriages and horses. This it was very easy to do, so long as they had the bottle in their possession; for Kokua was more bold than Keawe, and, whenever she had a mind, called on the imp for twenty or a hundred dollars. At this rate they soon grew to be remarked in the town; and the strangers from Hawaii, their riding and their driving, the fine holokus, and the rich lace of Kokua, became the matter of much talk.

They got on well after the first with the Tahiti language, which is indeed like the Hawaiian, with a change of certain letters; and as soon as they had any freedom of speech, began to push the bottle. You are to consider it was not an easy subject to introduce; it is not easy to persuade people you are in earnest when you offer to sell them for four centimes the spring of health and riches inexhaustible. It was necessary besides to explain the dangers of the bottle; and either people disbelieved the whole thing and laughed, or they thought the more of the darker part, became overcast with gravity, and drew away from Keawe and Kokua, as from persons who had dealings with the devil. So far from gaining ground, these two began to find they were avoided in the town; the children ran away from them screaming, a thing intolerable to Kokua; Catholics crossed themselves as they went by; and all persons began with one accord to disengage themselves from their advances.

Depression fell upon their spirits. They would sit at night in their new house, after a day's weariness, and not exchange one word, or the silence would be broken by Kokua bursting suddenly into sobs. Sometimes they would pray together; sometimes they would have the bottle out upon the floor, and sit all evening watching how the shadow hovered in the midst. At such times they would be afraid to go to rest. It was long ere slumber came to them, and, if either dozed off, it would be to wake and find the other silently weeping in the dark, or, perhaps, to wake alone, the other having fled from the house and the neighborhood of that bottle, to pace under the bananas in the little garden, or to wander on the beach by moonlight.

One night it was so when Kokua awoke. Keawe was gone. She felt in the bed and his place was cold. Then fear fell upon her, and she sat up in bed. A little moonshine filtered through the shutters. The room was bright, and she could spy the bottle on the floor. Outside it blew high, the great trees of the avenue cried aloud, and the fallen leaves rattled in the veranda. In the midst of this Kokua was aware of another sound; whether of a beast or of a man she could scarce tell, but it was as sad as death, and cut her to the soul. Softly she arose, set the door ajar, and looked forth into the moonlit yard. There, under the bananas, lay Keawe, his mouth in the dust, and as he lay he moaned.

It was Kokua's first thought to run forward and console him; her second potently withheld her. Keawe had borne himself before his wife like a brave man; it became her little in the hour of weakness to intrude upon his shame. With the thought she drew back into the house.

"Heaven," she thought, "how careless have I been—how weak! It is he, not I, who stands in this eternal peril; it was he, not I, who took the curse upon his soul. It is for my sake, and for the love of a creature of so little worth and such poor help, that he now beholds so close to him the flames of hell—ay, and smells the smoke of it, lying there in the wind and moonlight. Am I so dull of spirit that never till now I have surmised my duty, or have I seen it before and turned aside? But now, at least, I take up my soul in both the hands of my affection; now I say farewell to the white steps of heaven and the waiting faces of my friends. A love for a love, and let mine be equaled with Keawe's! A soul for a soul, and be it mine to perish!"

She was a deft woman with her hands, and was soon appareled. She took in her hands the charge—the precious centimes they kept ever at their side; for this coin is little used, and they had made provision at a government office. When she was forth in the avenue clouds came on the wind, and the moon was blackened. The town slept, and she knew not whither to turn till she heard someone coughing in the shadow of the trees.

"Old man," said Kokua, "what do you here abroad in the cold night?"

The old man could scarce express himself for coughing, but she made out that he was old and poor, and a stranger in the island.

"Will you do me a service?" said Kokua. "As one stranger to another, and as an old man to a young woman, will you help a daughter of Hawaii?"

"Ah," said the old man. "So you are the witch from the Eight Islands, and even my old soul you seek to entangle. But I have heard of you, and defy your wickedness."

"Sit down here," said Kokua, "and let me tell you a tale." And she told him the story of Keawe from the beginning to the end.

"And now," said she, "I am his wife, whom he bought with his soul's welfare. And what should I do? If I went to him myself and offered to buy it, he will refuse. But if you go, he will sell it eagerly; I will await you here; you will buy it for four centimes, and I will buy it again for three. And the Lord strengthen a poor girl!"

"If you meant falsely," said the old man, "I think God would strike you dead."

"He would!" cried Kokua. "Be sure He would. I could not be so treacherous; God would not suffer it."

"Give me the four centimes and await me here," said the old man.

Now, when Kokua stood alone in the street, her spirit died. The wind roared in the trees, and it seemed to her the rushing of the flames of hell; the shadows towered in the light of the street lamp, and they seemed to her the snatching hands of evil ones. If she had had the strength, she must have run away, and if she had had the breath, she must have screamed aloud; but, in truth, she could do neither, and stood and trembled in the avenue, like an affrighted child.

Then she saw the old man returning, and he had the bottle in his hand.

"I have done your bidding," said he. "I left your husband weeping like a child; tonight he will sleep easy." And he held the bottle forth.

"Before you give it to me," Kokua panted, "take the good with the evil—ask to be delivered from your cough."

"I am an old man," replied the other, "and too near the gate of the grave to take a favor from the devil. But what is this? Why do you not take the bottle? Do you hesitate?"

"Not hesitate!" cried Kokua. "I am only weak. Give me a moment. It is my hand resists, my flesh shrinks back from the accursed thing. One moment only!"

The old man looked upon Kokua kindly. "Poor child!" said he. "You fear: your soul misgives you. Well, let me keep it. I am old, and can never more be happy in this world, and as for the next——"

"Give it to me!" gasped Kokua. "There is your money.

Do you think I am so base as that? Give me the bottle."

"God bless you, child," said the old man.

Kokua concealed the bottle under her holoku, said farewell to the old man, and walked off along the avenue, she cared not whither. For all roads were now the same to her, and led equally to hell. Sometimes she walked, and sometimes ran; sometimes lay by the wayside in the dust and wept. All that she had heard of hell came back to her; she saw the flames blaze, and she smelled the smoke, and her flesh withered on the coals.

Near day she came to her mind again, and returned to the house. It was even as the old man said—Keawe slumbered like a child. Kokua stood and gazed upon his face.

"Now, my husband," said she, "it is your turn to sleep. When you wake it will be your turn to sing and laugh. But for poor Kokua, alas! that meant no evil—for poor Kokua no more sleep, no more singing, no more delight, whether in earth or heaven."

With that she lay down in the bed by his side, and her misery was so extreme that she fell in a deep slumber instantly.

Late in the morning her husband woke her and gave her the good news. It seemed he was silly with delight, for he paid no heed to her distress, ill though she dissembled it. The words stuck in her mouth, it mattered not; Keawe did the speaking. She ate not a bite, but who was to observe it? For Keawe cleared the dish. Kokua saw and heard him, like some strange thing in a dream; there were times when she forgot or doubted, and put her hands to her brow; to know herself doomed and hear her husband babble seemed so monstrous.

All the while Keawe was eating and talking, and planning the time of their return, and thanking her for saving him and fondling her, and calling her the true helper after all. He laughed at the old man who was fool enough to buy that bottle.

"A worthy man he seemed," Keawe said. "But no one can judge by appearances. For why did the old reprobate require the bottle?"

"My husband," said Kokua humbly, "his purpose may have been good."

Keawe laughed like an angry man.

"Fiddle-de-dee!" cried Keawe. "An old rogue, I tell you; and an old ass to boot. For the bottle was hard enough to sell at four centimes; and at three it will be quite impossible. The margin is not broad enough, the thing begins to smell of scorching—brrr!" said he, and shuddered. "It is true I bought it myself at a cent, when I knew not there were smaller coins. I was a fool for my pains; there will never be found another, and whoever has that bottle now will carry it to the pit."

"O my husband!" said Kokua. "Is it not a terrible thing to save oneself by the eternal ruin of another? It seems to me I could not laugh. I would be humbled. I would be filled with melancholy. I would pray for the poor holder."

Then Keawe, because he felt the truth of what she said, grew the more angry. "Heighty-teighty!" cried he. "You may be filled with melancholy if you please. It is not the mind of a good wife. If you thought at all of me, you would sit shamed."

Thereupon he went out, and Kokua was alone.

What chance had she to sell that bottle at two cen-times? None, she perceived. And if she had any, here was her husband hurrying her away to a country where there was nothing lower than a cent. And here—on the morrow of her sacrifice—was her husband leaving her and blaming her.

She would not even try to profit by what time she had, but sat in the house, and now had the bottle out and viewed it with unutterable fear, and now, with loathing hid it out of sight.

By and by Keawe came back, and would have her take a drive.

"My husband, I am ill," she said. "I am out of heart. Excuse me, I can take no pleasure."

Then was Keawe more wroth than ever. With her, because he thought she was brooding over the case of the old man; and with himself, because he thought she was right and was ashamed to be so happy.

"This is your truth," cried he, "and this your affec-tion! Your husband is just saved from eternal ruin, which he encountered for the love of you—and you can take no pleasure! Kokua, you have a disloyal heart."

He went forth again furious, and wandered in the town all day. He met friends, and drank with them; they hired a carriage and drove into the country, and there drank again. All the time Keawe was ill at ease, because he was taking this pastime while his wife was sad, and because he knew in his heart that she was more right than he; and the knowledge made him drink the deeper.

Now there was an old brutal Haole drinking with him,

one who had been a boatswain of a whaler—a runaway,
a digger in gold mines, a convict in prisons. He had a low
mind and a foul mouth; he loved to drink and to see
others drunken; and he pressed the glass upon Keawe.
Soon there was no more money in the company.

"Here, you!" says the boatswain. "You are rich, you
have been always saying. You have a bottle or some
foolishness."

"Yes," says Keawe, "I am rich; I will go back and get
some money from my wife, who keeps it."

"That's a bad idea, mate," said the boatswain. "Never
you trust a petticoat with dollars. They're all as false as
water; you keep an eye on her."

Now this word struck in Keawe's mind; for he was
muddled with what he had been drinking.

"I should not wonder but she was false indeed,"
thought he. "Why else should she be so cast down at my
release? But I will show her I am not the man to be
fooled. I will catch her in the act."

Accordingly, when they were back in town, Keawe
bade the boatswain wait for him at the corner by the
old calaboose, and went forward up the avenue alone
to the door of his house. The night had come again;
there was a light within, but never a sound; and Keawe
crept about the corner, opened the back door softly, and
looked in.

There was Kokua on the floor, the lamp at her side;
before her was a milk-white bottle, with a round belly
and a long neck; and as she viewed it, Kokua wrung her
hands.

A long time Keawe stood and looked in the doorway.

At first he was struck stupid; and then fear fell upon him that the bargain had been made amiss, and the bottle had come back to him as it came at San Francisco; and at that his knees were loosened, and the fumes of the wine departed from his head like mists off a river in the morning. And then he had another thought; and it was a strange one that made his cheeks to burn.

"I must make sure of this," thought he.

So he closed the door, and went softly round the corner again, and then came noisily in, as though he were but now returned. And, lo! by the time he opened the front door no bottle was to be seen; and Kokua sat in a chair and started up like one awakened out of sleep.

"I have been drinking all day and making merry," said Keawe. "I have been with good companions, and now I only came back for money, to return to drink and carouse with them again."

Both his face and voice were as stern as judgment, but Kokua was too troubled to observe.

"You do well to use your own, my husband," said she, and her words trembled.

"Oh, I do well in all things," said Keawe, and he went straight to the chest and took out money. But he looked besides in the corner where they kept the bottle, and there was no bottle there.

At that the chest heaved upon the floor like a sea billow, and the house spun about him like a wreath of smoke, for he saw she was lost now, and there was no escape. "It is what I feared," he thought. "It is she who has bought it."

And then he came to himself a little and rose up; but

the sweat streamed on his face as thick as the rain and as cold as the well water.

"Kokua," said he, "I said to you today what ill became me. Now I return to carouse with my jolly campanions," and at that he laughed a little quietly. "I will take more pleasure in the cup if you forgive me."

She clasped his knees in a moment, she kissed his knees with flowing tears.

"Oh," she cried, "I ask but a kind word!"

"Let us never think hardly of the other," said Keawe, and was gone out of the house.

Now, the money that Keawe had taken was only some of that store of centime pieces they had laid in at their arrival. It was very sure he had no mind to be drinking. His wife had given her soul for him, now he must give his for hers; no other thought was in the world with him.

At the corner, by the old calaboose, there was the boatswain waiting.

"My wife has the bottle," said Keawe, "and, unless you help me to recover it, there can be no more money and no more liquor tonight."

"You do not mean to say you are serious about that bottle?" cried the boatswain.

"There is the lamp," said Keawe. "Do I look as if I was jesting?"

"That is so," said the boatswain. "You look as serious as a ghost."

"Well, then," said Keawe, "here are two centimes; you just go to my wife in the house, and offer her these for the bottle, which (if I am not much mistaken) she will give you instantly. Bring it to me here, and I will buy it back from you for one; for that is the law with this bottle, that it still must be sold for a less sum. But whatever you do, never breathe a word to her that you have come from me."

"Mate, I wonder are you making a fool of me?" asked the boatswain.

"It will do you no harm if I am," returned Keawe.

"That is so, mate," said the boatswain.

"And if you doubt me," added Keawe, "you can try. As soon as you are clear of the house, wish to have your pocket full of money, or a bottle of the best rum, or what you please, and you will see the virtue of the thing."

"Very well, Kanaka," says the boatswain. "I will try; but if you are having your fun out of me, I will take my fun out of you with a belaying pin."

So the whaleman went off up the avenue; and Keawe stood and waited. It was near the same spot where Kokua had waited the night before; but Keawe was more resolved, and never faltered in his purpose; only his soul was bitter with despair.

It seemed a long time he had to wait before he heard a voice singing in the darkness of the avenue. He knew the voice to be the boatswain's; but it was strange how drunken it appeared upon a sudden.

Next the man himself came stumbling into the light of the lamp. He had the devil's bottle buttoned in his coat; another bottle was in his hand; and even as he came in view he raised it to his mouth and drank.

"You have it," said Keawe. "I see that."

"Hands off!" cried the boatswain, jumping back. "Take a step near me, and I'll smash your mouth. You thought you could make a catspaw of me, did you?"

"What do you mean?" cried Keawe.

"Mean?" cried the boatswain. "This is a pretty good bottle, this is; that's what I mean. How I got it for two centimes I can't make out; but I am sure you shan't have it for one."

"You mean you won't sell?" gasped Keawe.

"No, sir," cried the boatswain. "But I'll give you a drink of the rum, if you like."

"I tell you," said Keawe, "the man who has that bottle goes to hell."

"I reckon I'm going anyway," returned the sailor. "And this bottle's the best thing to go with I've struck yet. No, sir!" he cried again. "This is my bottle now, and you can go and fish for another."

"Can this be true?" Keawe cried. "For your own sake, I beseech you, sell it to me!"

"I don't value any of your talk," replied the boatswain. "You thought I was a flat, now you see I'm not; and there's an end. If you won't have a swallow of the rum, I'll have one myself. Here's your health, and good night to you!"

So off he went down the avenue towards town, and there goes the bottle out of the story.

But Keawe ran to Kokua light as the wind; and great was their joy that night; and great, since then, has been the peace of all their days in the Bright House.

My Displaced Ghosts
by JOHN WEST

You probably haven't heard of the D.G. problem yet. It's just begun to develop, but it's getting bigger all the time. If you come home some night and find your neat little split-level ranch-type house occupied by a strange spook, don't be surprised.

You won't like it, of course. But neither will the ghost. A ghost likes privacy as much as people do. Maybe more. But the way things are going, if a ghost does show up, you're going to have to live with it.

D.G. simply stands for Displaced Ghosts. All over the country, big old houses, many of them empty and rundown, are being wrecked. These are the kinds of houses ghosts like to haunt. In their place are being built acre after acre of small, compact, three-bedroom jobs. Ghosts hate small houses. But with the big houses being torn down every place you turn, where else is there for the ghosts to go?

I stumbled onto the D.G. problem because I owned a big, rambling, rundown old house north of Los Angeles, California. It was a fine old Spanish-style mansion built along the crest of a ridge that gave it a wonderful view of the hills. It was one of a group of six, all pretty much alike, with big stables and outbuildings, built back about 1880 by six rich men from the East, who decided to spend their days in California and wanted to stay together.

They liked privacy, so they built a long way from anybody else. They had enough money to buy up the land around them, and they imported servants, so for a few years they lived in grand style.

Well, times changed. Since the war money has been tight and servants scarce, and the descendants of the original six found the location too lonely for them.

One by one the big houses were deserted. The only reason I lived there was because I had inherited one of the houses from an elderly uncle. And I'm a writer. I don't make much money. I needed a place to live and the big old mansion was a roof over my head.

In the beginning, I just sort of camped there, and it was pretty lonely. Then I learned my house had a ghost in it. The ghost waited for about six months before letting me see him, then one night when I was at my typewriter, he materialized slowly in the air in front of me.

I won't go into the details. I mean about my hair standing on end, and feeling cold chills and all that. Because none of it happened. The truth is, I was feeling so lonely at the moment that even a ghost was welcome. I jumped up and tried to shake his hand, and all I could manage was the feel as if I had touched a wet fish very fast.

But that was all right. He understood. He was the ghost of a Spanish grandee named Don Estaban y Garcia, who had been killed in a duel on that spot two hundred years before. A real gentleman. Gentleghost I should say.

He had been haunting the house ever since it had been built. He'd never caused any trouble; most ghosts don't, you know. They're rather considerate people. I mean phantoms. It's only the unhappy ghosts, or the ones with bad consciences, that go around moaning and groaning and scaring people.

Many was the night, Don Esteban told me, that he had attended a big party in the house without ever being suspected. He merely moved around unseen, breathing the aroma of the gentlemen's cigars, sniffing the fragrance of the ladies' perfume, occasionally inhaling a deep whiff from a glass of brandy, and thoroughly enjoying himself. He would have been ashamed of himself to have alarmed anyone.

Don Esteban had only shown himself to me because

he could feel I was lonely. Also, I was getting a bit desperate about my writing. No sales; no money. He hoped I might forgive him. He only wanted to help if he could. Maybe a little company—even ghostly company—would cheer me up.

As soon as I got used to the idea, I began to appreciate his thoughtfulness. It gave me somebody to talk to, you know. A writer needs to talk. He likes to try out his plots. Esteban was willing to listen to me all night.

The trouble was, he didn't like my material. He kept shaking his head.

I should write about real people, he told me. For instance—and he started off on a tale of his ancestors who had come exploring in California with the early missionaries.

Adventure? Romance? It was the real thing, and I knew it. I wrote it down, making only a few changes, and rushed it off to New York. A couple of weeks later I got my first real check, and I decided to throw a party to celebrate—after using most of the money to pay up my back taxes.

There weren't any people living close enough to come to a party, so I decided it would just be for Don Esteban and myself. I set the table in the big old dining room with the paneled walls. Real linen tablecloth, real silver, real crystal wine glasses—I'd inherited them all from my late uncle, but never had a use for them before.

When everything was ready, I poured some wine, lit a fine cigar, and let it burn in an ashtray. Then I lit the candles and called Don Esteban. I had to call several times, and when he finally did materialize, he only half made it. I mean, he materialized from his waist up, and floated there, looking at me sheepishly.

"Don Esteban!" I said. "It's a party! Come on! Shape your essence and sit down! Sniff the cigar—imported from Spain. And the champagne. France's best!"

With an effort he finished himself as far as his knees. He couldn't seem to manage his legs and feet. Perhaps because the polished boots he wore were rather hard to materialize.

"What is it, Don Esteban?" I asked. He wasn't himself at all. "Something wrong?"

"I have a confession to make, amigo," he said, in a very small voice. Of course, ghosts seldom have really loud voices, but this was just a whisper.

"A confession?" I couldn't imagine what he was getting at. "What kind of confession?"

"There are others of us present," he said. He held himself erect, like a true Spanish grandee. "I—I have abused your hospitality, amigo. This last week or so I have been giving refuge under your roof to a number of D.G.'s."

"D.G.'s?" I stared at him, baffled. "I've heard of D. T.'s but what are D.G.'s?"

"Displaced ghosts," Don Esteban said sadly. Then he went on to tell me about the displaced ghost problem. I've already filled you in on the details. Big houses being torn down, resident ghosts with no place to go—— Well, the long and short of it was that Don Esteban had allowed a few of them to come to haunt my house.

"I realize I shouldn't have done it, amigo," he said. "It is, after all, a matter of pride with us never to haunt in groups. Sometimes, in the case of castles, we may allow two or even three ghosts to haunt it, but a house such as yours——No, I have done wrong! I humbly apologize. I will send them away."

"Now wait a minute, Don Esteban," I said. I was feeling good about the sale I had just made. "This is a big house and another ghost or two—I probably won't mind it. Why don't you just introduce your friends and let's talk this over."

"Very well," he said. "Let me introduce Señorita Marguerita Velasquez. Unfortunately caught in a landslide up in Santa Barbara in 1851. Her home, a big one, is but one of many that have just fallen into the hands of the wreckers."

The señorita materialized about three feet off the floor and gave a curtsy. She was—I mean she had been a very good-looking señorita.

"I thank you, señor," she said in a charming almost-voice, "for giving us sanctuary. And my mother thanks you. My father thanks you. My two brothers thank you. My sister thanks you."

"Tell them they are welcome, when you write," I said grandly. "They're back in Spain, I suppose?"

"Oh, no." I had the positive feeling she was trying to blush, but it is very hard to tell when a ghost is blushing. I mean, a blush is caused by blood rushing to the surface of the skin and ghosts don't have any blood. You can see the problem. But as I say, she tried.

"They are here with me, señor. We were all caught in the same landslide."

And like those Japanese paper flowers you put in a

glass of water, just tiny pellets that bloom into full-sized flowers, her whole family materialized in front of me . . . papa, mama, sister, and two great big brothers, all of them aristocrats.

Now instead of just Don Esteban, I had seven ghosts in the house with me. I was beginning to feel a little crowded.

"Don Esteban—" I gave him a look that made him disappear from the waist down—"I'm beginning to understand what you mean by the D.G. problem. All these folks—phantoms, I mean—are displaced ghosts?"

He nodded, slowly materializing his lower half again. This time he managed his feet, polished boots and all.

"All from Santa Barbara," he said. "Unfortunately, a whole group of old houses there is being torn down by the developers. However, amigo, these are all. Absolutely all—unless you count the players."

"Count the players?" I asked. "You sound like someone selling a baseball program! Buy a program and count the players! What the deuce do you mean, the players?"

"I mean the theatrical troupe, the traveling actors—players, as they were formerly called. You see, there were two stagecoaches going through a pass in Santa Barbara that year. One carried Señorita Marguerita Velasquez and her family, the other carried the players, bound for San Francisco. Alas, the same landslide took them all, without partiality. I will introduce them!"

I took a glass of the wine I had poured, to steady my nerves. After all, ghosts are ghosts. I mean nothing to be scared of, but a whole roomful can make you nervous. I hate crowds, anyway.

"Sir Anthony Trembleau," Don Esteban said, like an announcer at a big party. "Lady Trembleau. The Right Honorable Anthony Mainwaring. Miss Cynthia Lovelace. Richard Trent. Howard Lamb. John and Will Jameson. . ."

With every name he spoke, a new spook appeared. Some stood on the floor, some floated in the air. Sir Anthony Trembleau was a fine-looking gentleman with flashing eyes. His wife was a very strong-willed looking lady. The others—well, they were all actors. They were all dressed in full Shakespearean costumes. For *Hamlet,* I believe. Altogether there were eleven of them. Plus the other seven. Eighteen ghosts in all.

"You're positive this is all?" I asked Don Esteban. He nodded, then disappeared up to his chin. As he materialized I realized he was hiding something from me.

"All right," I sighed. "Where are the others?"

"Oh, not in the house, amigo," he said. "Come to the window."

I went to the window with him. We both leaned out. Don Esteban put his fingers between his lips and gave a ghostly whistle.

Then out of my garage, which had once been the stables for the big house, came a ghostly stagecoach, pulled by four phantom horses. Behind it came a second coach, larger and pulled by six equine spooks. The two coaches marched around the back yard and returned to the stables.

"The coach, the coachmen and helpers, and the horses, amigo," Don Esteban said. "Naturally, they have to haunt the stables."

He felt me looking at him, and he sighed.

"I am sorry," he said. "It was very necessary. The D.G. problem is becoming acute and this house is so suitable."

I took some more wine. My nerves were steadier but my knees were feeling wobbly.

"Don Esteban," I said, being very stern, "send them away. There are five other empty houses in this group. All big. All empty. All echoey and dark and spooky. Send your friends to haunt those houses and you can visit them, nights."

Don Esteban vanished all the way up to his eyes. He was embarrassed. And suddenly I knew the truth.

"Don Esteban!" I yelled at him. "Have you gone and filled those other houses with displaced ghosts, too?"

Slowly he reappeared and nodded.

"All," he said. "There are cowboys and Indians, dudes, several fine folk who became ghosts during the San Francisco fire of 1906, gold miners, hunters—I don't know who all. Some of them are rough diamonds. Their manners are not of the best. I invited only the quality ghosts to your residence, amigo."

I fainted.

I have no doubt that it was a faint. I came to on my own bed, fully clothed, next morning, and assumed Don Esteban and his friends had managed to carry me there. I had a splitting headache. The result, of course, of realizing that I not only harbored eighteen ghosts in my home, but was surrounded by other empty houses jammed to the rafters with ghost refugees.

Why, I couldn't take a step now without feeling watched. I kept stopping and stepping aside, feeling I was about to bump into some unseen ghost. I didn't dare sit down for fear of sitting on a phantom.

I couldn't write any more. I couldn't eat. Soon I was a wreck, a mere shell of my former self.

Don Esteban tried to talk to me a few times, but I couldn't bear the sight of him any more. I began to feel —yes, I actually began to feel prejudiced toward ghosts! Cold chills ran up and down my back and my hair stood on end when Don Esteban approached.

It wasn't my fault. I couldn't help myself. Eighteen ghosts in one house are a lot of phantoms to have to live with. Especially after they started to quarrel. About who was going to haunt which room and at what hours. The whole house was filled with ghostly footsteps, ghostly bangings and stampings, sighs, groans, moans, and other assorted phantasmal sound effects.

If I'd had the money, I'd have gone some place else. Any place else.

Then the State Highway Department came to my rescue.

You probably know that California has more people than any other state in the Union. Also more automobiles. Also more roads. California is constantly building new roads for new people with new automobiles. In California they are called freeways. And all the freeways are jammed. No matter how many new ones are built.

Well, one day some engineers came through my region, surveying. They told me a freeway was going right smack through the spot where my old house stood. The house would have to come down. I'd be paid for it, of course. I could have kissed them on the spot. But I didn't. They wouldn't have understood.

Now that I knew I could unload that old house for a good price, I became cheerful again. I even stopped resenting Don Esteban and his phantom friends. I stayed up evenings and let them haunt me.

We had some nice chats. The Shakespearean troupe of players did a complete version of *Hamlet* in the library. Hamlet's father's ghost played by a real ghost was a wow. They did *Macbeth,* too. That has a ghost in it—Banquo's ghost. Of course, having a ghost play a ghost is type casting, but it certainly was effective. I applauded for five minutes, while they took bows. They all felt better than they had for years, they told me.

Actors are actors, dead or alive. They yearn for applause.

Naturally, I kept the news about the sale of the house to myself. In a way I felt badly that the house was going to be demolished and all my D.G. boarders were going to be displaced still again. Now that I had got to know them better, I actually began to like them. They had a spooky sort of charm. But it was too late to do anything about it anyway.

When a state Highway Department decides to build a road, that's it. Anything in the way comes down. And besides, I'd already signed the initial papers and the other houses had been happily unloaded by their absentee owners.

Since the ghosts never stirred before nightfall, they weren't aware of all the activity. Don Esteban didn't learn what was about to happen until the day the Project Chief and his assistant came to the house to have me sign the last papers.

They were delayed and didn't get there until after dark. I should have realized that this could mean trouble, but I didn't. I was looking forward to getting that nice fat check from the Highway Department.

I tried to hurry the Project Chief and his assistant, a young chap named Harry, through the details, but they weren't in any rush. We had to sit in the library and smoke cigars while they talked about what the new freeway was going to mean to the state.

"Just think," the Project Chief said, letting his gaze roam around the room. "All these old houses will be cleaned out and a lovely eight-lane highway will run through here. Eight lanes of the finest concrete, with the most up-to-date road markers on it, capable of carrying——" He turned to his assistant. "How many cars will it carry, Harry?"

"Ten thousand cars an hour, peak load," Harry said. "Figuring an average speed of sixty miles an hour, that is."

"Ten thousand cars an hour, all doing sixty, right over this spot. It certainly must make you feel good to think about that," the Project Chief said happily. "All those people, going from one place to another, and then going back again. And it's us—Harry and me and the others—who make it possible. I tell you, sir, it warms our hearts to meditate upon it."

"Well, now, I see your point," I told him. "You'll probably want to be running along, to get yourself a motel before it's too late. I would invite you to stay here, but I haven't any sheets, blankets, things like that."

"Yes, I guess we'd better go. Come along, Harry," said the Project Chief, and they rose.

"It's been a pleasure to do business with you, Mr. West," he said to me. "You can leave any time now—officially, this house now belongs to the State. I estimate we'll have it torn down in six weeks. I wouldn't waste too much time getting anything you want to save out of it."

He let his eyes roam over the fine old redwood paneling.

"Shame to have to rip out all this fine old woodwork," he murmured. "But that's progress for you."

That's when Don Esteban y Garcia appeared. Standing beside the fireplace, fixing me with a haunting stare. He looked ghastly. I mean ghostly. No, I don't know what I mean. Just that he looked awful. If a ghost could turn pale, Don Esteban had turned pale. His eyes glared.

"Good heavens!" the Project Chief cried. "What's that?"

Don Esteban faded out, all except his eyes, which fixed me with one last accusing stare before they, too, disappeared.

"Nothing," I said. "Nothing at all."

I had my first premonition of trouble coming. The way Don Esteban had looked at me—you'd think I'd stabbed him in the back or something. I decided on the spot not to stay in that house one more night. Not with so many ghosts who, it suddenly occurred to me, might be resentful.

"Gentlemen," I said, "I believe I'll come with you. To the motel. My car is being fixed so if you can give me a lift——"

They were glad to. I was packed and out of there in five minutes. As I went, I had the feeling of being watched. By unseen shapes. All of them furious at me.

It was a relief when the Project Chief's station wagon started down the private road that connected the six old houses.

"Yessirree!" he said, looking around him as he drove. "Eight lanes of pure concrete running right over this spot! It'll be the finest road in the country when it's finished. Take the traffic pressure off the Coast Highway."

He'd hardly said that when my worst fears were realized.

I'd guessed Don Esteban would try something, but I thought that if I could get away soon enough, I'd fool him and the others.

Obviously he'd been too fast for me.

Down the road straight for us at a dead gallop came an old-fashioned stagecoach, drawn by six horses. Chasing the coach was a band of mounted Indians, giving out shrieks to curdle the blood. Every last one of them a ghost, you understand. I recognized the coach. It came from my stable. The Indians must have come from the next house. Don Esteban had rounded them up fast.

The coach came careening toward us. It was filled with the Shakespearean acting troupe. They all leaned out the windows, registering extreme terror.

The Project Chief saw the coach about to crash into us and just gave a moan. He let go the wheel and covered his eyes with his hands. The car swerved off the road and overturned in a ditch just as the phantom stagecoach rushed past us, followed by the whooping Indians.

Luckily we hadn't been going more than ten miles an hour. We were jarred and jolted, but when we unscrambled ourselves and crawled out, we weren't hurt.

The Project Chief and his assistant looked numb. Dazed.

I didn't blame them. I was pretty shaken myself.

"What . . . was . . . that?" the Project Chief, a large portly man, asked spacing his words.

"I saw a stagecoach, chased by Indians, coming down the road at us," Harry, the young man, announced. He wiped his upper lip. "They ran right through us," he said.

"Good heavens, they're coming back!" the Project Chief cried.

He ducked behind the overturned station wagon. We joined him.

The coach came rushing back at us. Now the six phantom horses were breathing fire, a little touch someone had thought up in the interval.

So were the horses of the Indians. All breathing fire. Even though I knew it was just a lot of ghosts play-acting, I couldn't help feeling sorry for the Project Chief and Harry.

The Indians caught the stagecoach directly in front of us. They dragged out the ghostly Shakespearean troupe inside. They scalped every one of them while we watched. Of course, all the actors were wearing wigs. I saw Sir Anthony Trembleau wink at me as his Indian scalped off his wig.

After the performance was over, the whole scene just faded from view.

I helped two badly shaken men back to my old house —actually the State's old house now—and gave them something to revive them. It was half an hour and several revivals later before they could speak clearly. Then they demanded to know what was going on around there.

While I was trying to answer, Sir Anthony Trembleau materialized in front of us. Still in costume as Hamlet's uncle, you understand. But for a little added touch he was carrying his head under his arm. These actors! They'll do anything for an effect.

"Sir Anthony Trembleau, at your service, gentlemen," he said and made a bow. The effect of the bow was sadly marred by the fact that he dropped his head. The Project Chief staggered backwards. Harry, his assistant, caught him and they fell into a chair together.

"I am here in the public interest, sir." Sir Anthony now was talking directly to the Project Chief, in his best acting voice. "To save you from making a sad mistake. Do you not know that this ridge upon which these houses sit is known as—" he lowered his voice to a sepulchral whisper— "Haunted Hill'?"

"H-H-Haunted Hill?" The Project Chief was stuttering now. As I have said, he was a big man and every inch of him quivered.

"Did you say H-H-Haunted H-H-Hill?" squeaked Harry, like a stuttering echo.

"Haunted Hill. The valley down below, where all the trees are, is known as Spooky Hollow."

As he said this, Sir Anthony Trembleau gave a ghostly laugh. The Project Chief swallowed three times before he could speak.

"You're ghosts? You haunt this property?" he asked.

"We are spirits, sir, lady and gentlemen spirits. And we inhabit this property. If you wish to call it haunting, you may do so," Sir Anthony replied with—I almost said spirit.

The Project Chief sat up. He pushed Harry off his lap and Harry got his own chair. The Project Chief was beginning to recover himself. You have to be a tough man to be a Project Chief of a big highway development program. Any man who dispossesses real living people every day to get room to build new roads isn't going to be stopped by a mere ghost or two.

"My friend," he said, "this house is coming down. You will soon find a beautiful eight-lane freeway of the finest American-made white concrete, guaranteed to last fifty years, running where this house is. Then what will you and all the other spooks do? You won't have any house to haunt any more."

"Then, sir, we will haunt the freeway," said Sir

Anthony with dignity. "It will be known as the Haunted Highway. We will have stagecoach races nightly, followed by Indian attacks, and then by battles between cowboys and Indians. From dusk until dawn we will romp on your beautiful eight lanes of white concrete for a distance of two miles in each direction."

"You couldn't!" The Project Chief turned a ghostly off-white himself. "You wouldn't!"

"We could and we would!" said Sir Anthony. "Permit me to introduce you to my fellow spirits. First, Lady Trembleau!"

Lady Trembleau materialized. Then the rest of the Shakespearean troupe, each one bowing to the pop-eyed Project Chief and his assistant. Then Sir Anthony started materializing the family of Señorita Velasquez. He was starting in on the Indians and cowboys when I slipped from the room.

I went to my own room and called: "Don Esteban! Come here! Show yourself!"

Slowly Don Esteban materialized, right down to the pointed toes of his shiny boots. He seemed reproachful, yet self-satisfied.

"Amigo," he said, "I thought you were our friend. To think you would do this to me—to us! Sell the house to be torn down and make D.G.'s out of us!"

"I didn't do anything," I told him. "Listen, when a highway department gets a mad passion to push eight lanes of nice new concrete across your property, nothing human is going to stop them."

"We're not human," Don Esteban said. "We are spirits. We are making our last stand in this world of

123

progress, and we intend to fight with every weapon. We will haunt that new highway until frightened drivers by the hundreds pile up their shiny new cars and join us. It will be worse than a battlefield. It will be—catastrophe!"

"What's happened to you, Don Esteban?" I demanded. "You told me when we first met that ghosts are shy, that they don't like trouble, that they only show themselves when they have to!"

"It is the influence of the players, of Sir Anthony Trembleau and his company," Don Esteban said. "Every actor wants an audience, even if he is just a ghost of an actor. The little scene we staged outside an hour ago was directed by Sir Anthony, with some help from you."

"From me?" I cried. "How did I help?"

"Those trashy historical adventure stories you were trying to write when we first met," Don Esteban said. "They gave me all the material I needed to help Sir Anthony work out an impromptu script."

"Well!" I stared at him. An idea was beginning to come to me. "Listen, could you do it again, any time you wanted? That stagecoach chase? And others like it?"

"All night long," Don Esteban said. "If we had an audience. Sir Anthony and his troupe are turning us all into hams, I'm afraid."

"Then," I cried, "if you'll just play along with me— all of you—I may have the solution."

And I went back into the library, where the Project Chief and Harry were staring, eyes popping, lips trembling, knees shaking, at a room so packed with assorted ghosts that some of them were being squeezed into the fireplace and sucked up the chimney by the natural draft.

"Okay, boys, break it up," I said briskly. "I want to talk business to these gentlemen."

Don Esteban made a sign and the ghosts all vanished.

I poured a strong dose of revival medicine for the two men.

"Gentlemen," I said, "you have a problem. If you build this highway, it will be known as the Haunted Highway. Every evening will see a scene of carnage and massacre unrivaled since the sack of ancient Troy. And you—*you* will be blamed for engineering an unsafe highway. Because who will believe the drivers are being scared off the road by ghosts?"

"It's true, Chief," Harry groaned. "We'll be blamed for building a deathtrap."

"Last year I won the National Safety Award for building the world's safest highway," the Project Chief cried. "It's only a mile long and doesn't go any place and no one drives on it so there weren't any accidents, but that's beside the point. I'm known for building safe highways. I can't have a thing like this on my record."

"We'll move the freeway!" Harry said. "We'll put it the other side of the hill. Mister West, you can have your house back."

"Now wait a minute," I said. "If you do that it'll cost several million. You'll have to explain why you changed the plans. What will you say? Have you thought of that?"

"Yes, Harry, what will we say?" the Project Chief echoed.

"We'll say we did it to avoid some ghosts who——No." Harry gave a long sigh. "That won't work either. Frankly, Chief, I don't know what we'll say."

"Gentlemen, if I may make some suggestions, I think I can help you out of your problem," I said.

And then I began to talk.

At first they said no.

They said no a second time.

Then they thought of their reputations as highway engineers, and they finally said yes. We drew up the agreements on the spot.

So the Highway Department, instead of tearing down the six fine, if run-down, old buildings, carefully moved them a quarter mile downhill into a nice, spooky sort of hollow, with trees and a brook. They built a good exit and entrance road to the spot from the splendid new, eight-lane freeway they then built where the houses had been.

They threw in a fence around the property for good measure, and, of course, made sure I had clear title to the land down in Spooky Hollow—as I renamed it—and to the houses.

We are now busy on the final stages of my scheme.

We're going to be open nightly, from sunset to sunup. We'll put on ghostly stagecoach races, phantom combats between spectral cowboys and Indians, scenes from Shakespeare for the culture lovers, and a lot of other inspiring entertainment that Sir Anthony Trembleau and his cast of hundreds of stage-struck ghosts are busy rehearsing.

Yes, sir, when you come out this way next, you'll be

able to see the spirit world integrated into the world of progress. We're licking the D.G. problem, anyway at the local level.

I predict we will be a major tourist attraction, right up beside Disneyland and Marineland. As there is almost nothing to do in California at night, except for a few night baseball games, and we will be open all night long right beside a modern freeway, I anticipate fabulous business.

Look for our signs next time you're out this way.

What are we going to call our enterprise?

Why, GHOSTLAND, of course.

What else?

Faith, Hope and Charity
by IRVIN S. COBB

Just outside a sizable New Mexico town the second section of the fast through train coming from the Coast
made a short halt. Entering the stretch leading to the
yards, the engineer had found the signal set against him;
the track ahead was temporarily blocked.

It was a small delay, though. Almost at once the
semaphore, like the finger of a mechanical wizard, made
the warning red light vanish and a green light appear
instead; so, at that, the Limited got under way and

rolled on into the station for her regular stop.

But before she started up, four travelers quitted her. They got out on the off side, the side farthest away from the town, and that probably explains why none of the crew and none of the other passengers saw them getting out. It helps also to explain why they were not missed until quite some time later.

Their manner of leaving was decidedly unusual. First, one of the vestibule doors between the third sleeping car and the fourth sleeping car opened and the trap in the floor flipped up briskly under the pressure of an impatient foot on the operating lever. A brace of the departing ones came swiftly into view, one behind the other. True, there was nothing unusual about that. But as they stepped down on the earth they faced about and received the figure of a third person whose limbs dangled and whose head lolled back as they took the dead weight of him into their arms. Next there emerged the fourth and last member of the group, he being the one who had eased the limp figure of Number Three down the car steps into the grasp of his associates.

For a fractional space their shapes made a little huddle in the lee of the vestibule. Looking on, you might have guessed that there was a momentary period of indecision touching on the next step to be taken.

However, this muddle—if that was what it was—right away straightened itself out. Acting with movements which seemed difficult and awkward, the two burden bearers carried their unconscious load down the short embankment and deposited it on the cindery underfooting close against the flank of the slightly built-up right of way.

Number Four bent over the sprawled form and fumbled at it, shoving his hands into first one pocket and then another. In half a minute or less he straightened up and spoke to the remaining pair, at the same time using both hands to shove some article inside the vent of his waistcoat.

"I have got them," he said, speaking with a foreign accent. They pressed toward him, their hands extended.

"Not here and not yet, Señores," he said sharply. "First we make sure of the rest. First you do, please, as I do."

Thereupon he hopped nimbly up the shoulder of the roadbed and headed toward the rear of the halted train, slinking well in under the overhang of the Pullmans. His mates obeyed his example. They kept on until they had passed the tail coach, which was a combination coach, and then they stepped inward between the rails, still maintaining their single-file formation. Immediately the dusk swallowed them up.

There was something peculiar about the way each one of these three plodding pedestrians bore himself. The peculiarity was this: He bore himself like a person engaged in prayer—in a silent perambulating act of piety. His head was tucked in, his face turning neither to the right nor left; his eyes were set steadfastly forward as though upon some invisible goal, his hands clasped primly together in front of him.

Thus and so the marching three plodded on until the train, having got in motion, was out of sight beyond a curve in the approach to the station. Then they checked and came together in a clump, and then, had you been there, you would have understood the reason for their devotional pose. All three of them were wearing handcuffs.

The man who had spoken before unpalmed a key ring which he was carrying. Working swiftly even in the half-darkness, he made tests of the keys on the ring until he found the proper keys. He freed the wrists of his two fellows. Then one of them took the keys and unlocked his set of bracelets for him.

He, it would seem, was the most forethoughted of the trio. With his heel he kicked shallow gouges in the gritty soil beside the track and buried the handcuffs therein.

After that they briefly confabbed together, and the upshot of the confab was that, having matched for the possession of some object evidently held to be of great value, they separated forces.

One man set off alone on a detour to the southeast, which would carry him around the town. His late companions kept on in a general westerly direction, heading toward the desert which all that day they had been traversing. They footed it fast, as men might foot it who were fleeing for their lives and yet must conserve their strength. As a matter of fact, they were fleeing for their lives. So likewise the one from whom they had just parted was fleeing for his life.

It was partly by chance that these three had been making the transcontinental journey in company. Two of them, Lafitte the Frenchman, and Verdi the Italian who had Anglicized his name and called himself Green, met while lying in jail at San Francisco awaiting deportation to their respective countries. Within a space of a month each had been arrested as a refugee from justice; the formalities for extraditing the pair of them were swiftly completed.

So, to save trouble and expense; to kill, as it were, two birds with one stone, the authorities decided to send them together across to the eastern seaboard where, according to arrangements made by cable, they would be surrendered to police representatives coming from abroad to receive them and transport them back overseas. For the long trip to New York a couple of city detectives had them in custody.

When the train bearing the officers and their charges reached a junction in lower California where the main line connected with a branch line running south to the Mexican border, there came aboard a special agent of the Department of Justice who had with him a prisoner.

This prisoner was one Manuel Gaza, a Spaniard. He also recently had been captured and identified; and he also was destined for return to his own land. It was not by prior agreement that he had been retransferred at this junction point to the same train which carried the Italian and the Frenchman. It just happened so.

It having happened so, the man who had Gaza in tow lost no time in getting acquainted with his San Francisco brethren. For a number of reasons it seemed expedient to all the officers that from here on they should travel as a unit. Accordingly the special agent talked with the Pullman conductor and exchanged the reservations he previously had booked for a compartment adjoining the drawing room in which the four from the city were riding.

It was on a Friday afternoon that the parties united. Friday evening, at the first call for dinner, the three officers herded their three prisoners forward to the dining car, the passage of the sextet through the aisles causing some small commotion. Their advent into the diner created another little sensation.

Since it was difficult for the handcuffed aliens to handle knife and fork, they were given such food as might readily be eaten with a spoon or with the fingers—soups and omelets and soft vegetables and pie or rice pudding. The detectives ate fish. They shared between them a double order of imported kippers.

Presumably they were the only persons on the train who that day had chosen the kippered herrings. Shortly, the special agent was giving private thanks that his church prescribed no dietetic regulations for Friday, because within an hour or two after leaving the table, the San Francisco men were suffering from violent cramps—ptomaine poison had them helpless.

One seemed to be dangerously ill. That night near the border between California and Arizona he was taken off the train and carried to a hospital. During the wait at the station, a local physician dosed the second and lesser sufferer, whose name was McAvoy, and when he had been somewhat relieved, the doctor gave him a shot of something in the arm and said he ought to be up and about within twenty-four hours.

Through the night McAvoy slept in the lower berth of the compartment and the special agent sat up, with the communicating door open, to guard the aliens, who were bedded in the so-called drawing room.

Their irons stayed on their wrists; their lone warden was accepting no foolish odds against himself. He had taken the precaution to transfer the keys of the Frenchman's handcuffs and the Italian's handcuffs from McAvoy's keeping to his own, slipping them on his key ring, but this had been done in case McAvoy should become seriously ill en route and it should devolve upon him to make a lap of the journey single-handed.

Next morning McAvoy was much easier but he felt weak, he said, and drowsy. Given a full twelve hours of rest, though, he thought he would be able to go on guard when nightfall came.

So he lay in his berth, and the special agent occupied an end of the drawing-room sofa. The trapped fugitives sat smoking cigarettes, and when the officer was not too near, talking among themselves.

Mainly they talked in English, a language which Gaza the Spaniard and Lafitte the Frenchman spoke fairly well. Verdi or Green, as the case might be, had little English at his command, but Gaza, who had spent three years in Naples, spoke Italian; and so when Verdi used his own tongue, Gaza could interpret for the Frenchman's benefit. They were allowed to quit the drawing room only for meals.

When dinner hour came on that second evening of their trip, McAvoy was in a doze. So the Department of Justice man did not disturb him.

"Come on, boys," he said to the three aliens; "time to eat again."

He lined them up in front of him in the corridor and they started the regular processional. It was just at that moment that the train broke its rhythmic refrain and began to clack and creak and slow for that unscheduled stop outside that New Mexico town. By the time they had reached the second car on ahead, she'd almost stopped and was lurching and jerking.

In the vestibule beyond that second car the special agent was in the act of stepping across the iron floor lip of the connection when a particularly brisk joggle caused him to lose his hat. He gave a small exclamation and bent to recover it. Doing so, he jostled Gaza, the third man in the line and therefore the next to him.

The agile Spaniard was quick to seize his chance. He half turned, and bringing his chained wrists aloft, sent them down with all his might on the poll of the officer's unprotected skull. The victim of the assault never made a sound—just spraddled on his face and was dead to the world.

No outsider had been witness to the assault. No outsider came along during the few seconds which were required by the late prisoners to open an off-side car door and make their escape after the fashion which already has been described for you. Nobody missed them —for quite a while nobody did.

It wasn't until nearly nine o'clock, when McAvoy had roused up and rung for the porter and begun to ask questions, that a search was made and an alarm raised.

* * *

Penned up together through that day, the aliens had matched stories, one story against another. A common plight made them communicative; a common peril caused each to turn with morbid reiteration to his own fatal predicament.

Said the Frenchman to the Spaniard: "He"—indicating his recent cellmate, the Italian—"he knows how with me it stands. With him, I have talked. He speaks not so well the English but sometimes he understands it. Now you shall hear and judge for yourself how bad my situation is."

Graphically, this criminal sketched his past. He had been a Marseilles dock hand. He had killed a woman. She deserved killing, so he killed her. He had been caught, tried, convicted, condemned. While lying in prison, with execution day only a few weeks distant, he had made a getaway.

In disguise he had reached America and here had stayed three years. Then another woman, in a fit of jealousy, betrayed him to the police. He had been living with that woman; to her he had given his confidence. It would appear that women had been his undoing.

"Me, I am as good as dead already. And what a death!" A spasm of shuddering possessed him. "For me the guillotine is waiting. The devil invented it. It is so they go at you with that machine: They strap you flat upon a board. Face downward you are, but you can look up, you can see—that is the worst part. They fit your throat into a grooved shutter; they make it fast. You bring your head back; your eyes are drawn upward,

fascinated. Above you, waiting, ready, poised, your eyes
see the—the knife.''

"But only for a moment do you see it, my friend,''
said the Spaniard, in the tone of one offering comfort.
"Only a moment and then—*pouff*—all over!''

"A moment! I tell you it is an eternity. It must be an
eternity. Lying there, you must live a hundred lives, you
must die a hundred deaths. And then to have your head
taken off your body, to be all at once in two pieces. Me,
I am not afraid of most deaths. But that death by the
guillotine—ah-h!''

The Spaniard bent forward. He was sitting alone facing the other two, who shared a seat.

"Listen, Señor,'' he stated. "Compared with me, you
are the lucky one. True, I have not yet been tried—before they could try me I fled away out of that accursed
Spain of mine.''

"Not tried, eh?'' broke in the Frenchman. "Then you
have yet a loophole—a chance for escape; and I have
none. My trial, as I told you, is behind me.''

"You do not know the Spanish courts. It is plain you
do not, since you say that,'' declared the Spaniard.
"Those courts—they are greedy for blood. With them,
to my kind, there is not mercy; there is only punishment.

"And such a punishment! Wait until you hear. To me
when they get me before them they will say: 'The proof
is clear against you; the evidence has been thus and so.
You are adjudged guilty. You took a life, so your life
must be taken. It is the law.'

"Perhaps I say: 'Yes, but that life I took swiftly and in passion and for cause. For that one the end came in an instant, without pain, without lingering, yes, without warning. Since I must pay for it, why cannot I also be made to die very quickly without pain!'

"Will they listen? No, they send me to the garrote. To a great strong chair they tie you—your hands, your feet, your trunk. Your head is against a post, an upright. In that post is a collar—an iron band. They fit that collar about your neck. Then from behind you the executioner turns a screw.

"If he chooses he turns it slowly. The collar tightens, tightens, a knob presses into your spine. You begin to strangle. Oh, I have seen it myself! I know. You expire by inches! I am a brave man, Señores. When one's time comes, one dies. But oh, Señores, if it were any death but that! Better the guillotine than that! Better anything than that!"

He slumped back against the cushions, and rigors passed through him.

It was the Italian's turn. "I was tried in my absence," he explained to the Spaniard. "I was not even there to make my defense—I had thought it expedient to depart. Such is the custom of the courts in my country. They try you behind your back.

"They found me guilty, those judges. In Italy there is no capital punishment, so they sentenced me to life imprisonment. It is to that—that—I now return."

The Spaniard lifted his shoulders; the lifting was eloquent of his meaning.

"Not so fast," said the Italian. "You tell me you lived

once in Italy. Have you forgotten what life imprisonment for certain acts means in Italy? It means solitary
confinement. It means you are buried alive. They shut
you away from everyone in a tight cell. It is a tomb,
that is all. You see no one ever; you hear no voice ever.
If you cry out, no one answers. Silence, darkness, darkness, silence, until you go mad or die.

"Can you picture what that means to one of my race,
to an Italian who must have music, sunshine, talk with
his fellows, sight of his fellows? It is in his nature—he
must have these things or he is in torture, in constant
and everlasting torment. Every hour becomes to him a
year, every day a century, until his brain bursts asunder
inside his skull.

"Oh, they knew—those fiends who devised this thing
—what to an Italian is a million times worse than death
—any death. I am the most unfortunate one of the three
of us. My penalty is the most dreadful by far."

The others would not have it so. They argued the
point with him and with each other all through the day,
and twilight found their beliefs unshaken.

Then, under the Spaniard's leadership, came their
deliverance out of captivity. It was he who, on the toss-
up, won the revolver which they had taken from the
person of the senseless special agent. Also it was he who
suggested to the Italian that for the time being, at least,
they stick together. To this the Italian had agreed, the
Marseilles man, Lafitte, already having elected to go
on his own.

After the latter, heading east by south, had left them,
the Spaniard said reflectively:

"He is optimistic, that one, for all that he seemed so gloomy and downhearted today when speaking of that guillotine of his. He said he now had faith that he would yet dodge his fate. Five minutes after he is off that train he speaks of faith!"

"I cannot go quite so far," answered the Italian. "We are free, but for us there will be still a thousand dangers. So I have not much faith, but I have hope. And you, my friend?"

The Spaniard shrugged his shoulders. His shrug might mean yes or it might mean no. Perhaps he needed his breath. He was going at a jog-trot down the tracks, the Italian alongside him.

Take the man who had faith. Set down as he was in a country utterly strange to him, this one of the fugitives nevertheless made steady progress. He got safely around and by the New Mexico town. He hid in the chaparral until daybreak, then took to a highway running parallel with the railroad.

A "tin canner," which is what they were beginning to call an itinerant motor tourist in those parts, overtook him soon after sunup and gave him a lift to a small way station some forty miles down the line. There he boarded a local train—he had some money on him; not much money but enough—and undetected, he rode that train clear on through to its destination a hundred miles or so farther along.

Other local trains carried him across a corner of Colorado and clear across Kansas. Some forty-eight hours later, he was a guest in a third-rate hotel on a back street in Kansas City, Missouri.

He stayed in that hotel for two days and two nights, biding most of the time in his room on the top floor of the six-story building, going down only for his meals and for newspapers. The food he had to have; the newspapers gave him information, of a sort, of the hunt for the three fugitives. It was repeatedly stated that all three were believed to be fleeing together. That cheered Lafitte very much. It strengthened his faith.

But on the morning of his third day in this cheap hotel, when he came out of his room and went down the hall to ring for the elevator—there was only one passenger elevator in this hotel—he saw something. Passing the head of the stairs, which ended approximately midway of the stretch between the door of his room and the wattled iron door opening on the elevator well, he saw, out of the corner of one watchful eye, two men in civilian garb on the steps below him.

They had halted there. Whether they were coming up or going down there was no way of telling. It seemed to him that at sight of him they ducked slightly and made as if to flatten themselves back against the side wall.

He gave no sign of having seen them. He stilled an impulse to make a dash for it. Where was he to dash for, with the stairs cut off? He followed the only course open to him. Anyhow he told himself he might be wrong. Perhaps his nerves were misbehaving. Perhaps those two who seemed to be lurking just there behind him on those steps were not interested in him at all. He kept telling himself that while he was ringing the bell, while he was waiting for the car to come up for him.

The car did come up and, for a wonder, promptly; an old-fashioned car, creaky, musty. Except for its shirt-sleeved attendant, it was empty. As Lafitte stepped in, he glanced sideways over his shoulder, making the movement casual—no sight of those two fellows.

He rode down, the only passenger for that trip, so there were no stops on the descent. They reached the ground floor, which was the office floor. The elevator came to a standstill, then moved up a foot or so, then joltingly down six inches or so as the attendant, who was not expert, maneuvered to bring the sill of the car flush with the tiling of the lobby.

The delay was sufficiently prolonged for Lafitte to realize, all in a flash, he had not been wrong. Through the intervening grille of the shaft door he saw two more men who pressed close up to that door, who stared in at him, whose looks and poses were watchful, eager, prepared. Besides, Lafitte knew plainclothes men when he saw them.

Up above and here below, he was cut off. There still was a chance for him, a poor one but the only one. If he could shoot the elevator aloft quickly enough, check it at the third floor or the fourth, say, and hop out, he might make a successful dart for the fire escape at the rear of the hotel—provided the fire escape was not guarded. In the space of time that the elevator boy was jockeying the car, he thought of this, and having thought it, acted on it.

Swinging his fist from behind with all his might, he

hit that hapless fellow on the point of the jaw and deposited him, stunned and temporarily helpless, on his knees in a corner of the cage. Lafitte grabbed the lever, shoved it over hard, and up the shaft shot the car. Before he could get control of it, being unfamiliar with such mechanisms and in a panic besides, it was at the top of the house. But then he mastered it and made it reverse its course, and returning downward he pulled the lever, bringing it toward him.

That was the proper notion, that gentler manipulation, for now the car, more obedient, was crawling abreast of the third-floor level. It crept earthward, inch by inch, and without bringing it to a dead stop he jerked up the latch of the collapsible safety gate, telescoped the metal outer door back into its folded-up self, and stooping low because the gap was diminishing, he lunged forward.

Now that elevator boy was a quick-witted, high tempered Irish boy. He might be half dazed but his instincts of belligerency were not asleep. He told afterward how, automatically and indignantly functioning, he grabbed at the departing assailant and caught him by one leg and for a fleeting moment, before the other kicked free, retarded him.

But by all that was good and holy he swore he did not touch the lever. Being down on all fours at the rear side of the slowly sinking car, how could he touch it? Why, just at that precise fraction of a second the elevator should pick up full speed was a mystery to him—to everybody else, for that matter.

But pick up full speed it did. And the Irish boy cowered down and screamed an echo to a still louder scream than his, and hid his eyes from the sight of Lafitte, with his head outside and his body inside the elevator, being decapitated as completely and almost as neatly as though a great weighted knife had sheared him off at the neck.

Take the Spaniard and Italian: Steadily they traveled westward for nearly all of that night which followed their evacuation from the Limited. It put desirable distance between them and the spot where they had dumped the special agent down. Also it kept them warm. This was summertime but on the desert even summer nights are chilly and sometimes downright cold. Before dawn, they came on a freight train waiting on a siding. Its locomotive faced west. That suited their book.

They climbed nimbly aboard a flat and snuggled themselves down behind a barrier of farm implements. Here, breakfastless but otherwise comfortable, they rode until nearly midday. Then a brakeman found them. Harshly he ordered them to get out of there.

Immediately though, looking at them where they squatted half hidden, his tone softened, and he told them he'd changed his mind about it and they could stay aboard as long as they pleased. On top of this, he hurried forward as though he might have important news for the engine crew or somebody.

They chose to get off. They had noted the quick start as of recognition which the brakeman had given. They figured—and figured rightly—that by now the chase for them was on and that their descriptions had been telegraphed back and forth along the line. The train was traveling at least twenty miles an hour, but as soon as the brakeman was out of sight, they jumped for it, tumbling like shot rabbits down the slope of the right of way and bringing up jarred and shaken in the dry ditch at the bottom.

Barring bruises and scratches, Green had taken no hurt, but Gaza landed with a badly sprained ankle. With Green to give him a helping arm, he hobbled away from the railroad.

To get away from that railroad was their prime aim now. Choosing a course at random, they went north over the undulating waste lands and through the shimmering heat, toward a range of mottled high buttes rising on beyond.

It took them until deep into the afternoon to cover a matter roughly of five miles. By now, Gaza's lower left leg was elephantine in its proportions and every forced step he took meant a fresh stab of agony. He knew he could not go much farther. Green knew it too, and in his brain began shaping tentative plans. The law of self-preservation was one of the few laws for which he had respect. They panted from heat and from thirst and from weariness.

At the end of those five miles, having toiled laboriously up over a fold in the land, they saw close at hand, and almost directly below them, a 'dobe hut and, not quite so near at hand, a big flock of sheep. At the door of the cabin, a man in overalls was stripping the hide from a swollen dead cow.

Before they could dodge back below the sky line, he

saw them and stood up expectantly. There was nothing for them to do except to go toward him. At their slow approach, an expression of curiosity crept over his brown face and stayed there. He looked like a Mexican or possibly a half-breed Indian.

When Gaza, stumbling nearer, hailed him in English, he merely shook his head dumbly. Then Gaza tried him in Spanish and to that he replied volubly. For minutes they palavered back and forth; then the stranger served them with deep draughts from a water bottle swinging in the doorway with a damp sack over it. The water was lukewarm and bitterish-tasting but it was balm to their parched throats. Then he withdrew inside the little house and Gaza, for Green's benefit, translated into Italian what talk had passed.

"He says he is quite alone here, which is the better for us," explained the Spaniard, speaking swiftly. "He says that a week ago he came up from Old Mexico, seeking work. A gringo—a white man—gave him work. The white man is a sheepman. His home ranch is miles away. In a sheep wagon he brought this Mexican here and left him here in charge of that flock yonder, with provisions for a month.

"It will be three weeks then before the white man, his employer, comes again. Except for that white man, he knows nobody hereabouts. Until we came just now, he had seen no one at all. So he is glad to see us."

"And accounting for ourselves you told him what?" asked Green.

"I told him we were traveling across country in a car and that going down a steepness last night the car overturned and was wrecked and I crippled myself. I told him that, traveling light because of my leg, we started out to find some town, some house, and that, hoping to make a short cut, we left the road, but that since morning and until we blundered upon this camp, we had been quite lost in this ugly country. He believes me. He is simple, that one, an ignorant, credulous peon.

"But kind-hearted, that also is plain. For proof of it observe this." He pointed to the bloated, half-flayed carcass. "He says three days ago he found this beast— a stray from somewhere, he knows not where. So far as he knows there are no cattle droves in these parts— only sheep.

"She was sick, she staggered, she was dizzy and turned in circles as if blind, and froth ran from her mouth. There is a weed which does that to animals when they eat it, he says. So, hoping to make her well again he put a scrap of rope on her horns and led her here. But last night she died. So today he has been peeling her. Now he goes to make ready some food for us. He is hospitable, also, that one."

"And when we have eaten, then what? We can't linger here."

"Wait, please, Señor. To my mind already an idea comes." His tone was authoritative, confident. "First we fill our empty stomachs to give us strength, and then we smoke a cigarette, and while we smoke, I think. And then—we see."

On frijoles and rancid bacon and thin corn cakes and bad coffee, which the herder brought them on tin platters and in tin cups, they did fill their empty stomachs.

Then they smoked together, all three of them, smoking cigarettes rolled in corn-husk wrappers.

The Mexican was hunkered on his heels, making smoke rings in the still, hot air when Gaza, getting on his feet with difficulty, limped toward the doorway, gesturing to show that he craved another swig from the water bottle. When he was behind the other two, almost touching them, he drew the special agent's pistol and fired once and their host tumbled forward on his face and spraddled his limbs and quivered a bit and was still, with a bullet hole in the back of his head.

This killing gave the Italian, seasoned killer as he was, a profound shock. It seemed so unnecessary, unless ——? He started up, his features twitching, and backed away, fearing the next bullet would be for him.

"Remain tranquil, Señor," said the Spaniard, almost gayly. "For you, my comrade, there is no danger. There is for you hope of deliverance, you who professed last night to hope in your soul.

"Now me, I have charity in my soul—charity for you, charity for myself, charity also for this one lying here. Behold, he is now out of his troubles. He was a dolt, a clod of the earth, a creature of no refinement. He lived a hermit's life, lonely, miserable. Now he has been dispatched to a better and a brighter world. That was but kindness." With his foot he touched the sprawled corpse.

"But in dispatching him I had thought also for you—for both of us. I elucidate: First we bury him under the dirt floor of this house, taking care to leave no telltale traces of our work. Then you make a pack for your back of the food that is here. You take also the water bottle, filled. Furthermore, you take with you this pistol.

"Then, stepping lightly on rocky ground or on hard ground so that you make no tracks, you go swiftly hence and hide yourself in those mountains until—who can tell?—until those who will come presently here have ceased to search for you. With me along, lamed as I am, me to hamper you, there would be no chance for either of us. But you, going alone—you armed, provisioned, quick of foot—you have a hope."

"But—but you? What then becomes of you?—You— you sacrifice yourself?" In his bewilderment the Italian stammered.

"Me, I stay here to greet the pursuers. It is quite simple. In peaceful solitude I await their coming. It cannot be long until they come. That man of the freight train will be guiding them back to pick up our trail. By tonight at latest I expect them."

At sight of the Italian's mystified face he broke now into a laugh.

"Still you are puzzled, eh? You think that I am magnanimous, that I am generous? Well, all that I am. But you think me also a fool and there you err. I save you perhaps but likewise perhaps I save myself. Observe, Señor."

He stooped and lifted the dead face of his victim. "See now what I myself saw the moment I beheld this herder of ours: This man is much my shape, my height, my coloring. He spoke a corrupt Spanish such as I can speak. Put upon me the clothes which he wears, and remove from my lip this mustache which I wear, and I would pass for him even before the very eyes of that white man who hired him.

"Well, very soon I shall be wearing his clothes, my own being hidden in the same grave with him. Within ten minutes I shall be removing this mustache. He being newly shaven, as you see for yourself, it must be that in this hovel we will find a razor. I shall pass for him. I shall be this mongrel dull wit."

A light broke on the Italian. He ran and kissed the Spaniard on both cheeks and on the mouth.

"Ah, my brother!" he cried out delightedly. "Forgive me that for a moment I thought you hard-hearted for having in seeming wantonness killed the man who fed us. I see you are brilliant—a great thinker, a great genius. But, my beloved"—and here doubt once more assailed him—"what explanation do you make when they do come?"

"That is the best of all," said Gaza. "Before you leave me you take a cord and you bind me most securely—my hands crossed behind my back—so; my feet fastened together—so. It will not be for very long that I remain so. I can endure it. Coming then, they find me thus. That I am bound makes more convincing the tale I shall tell them.

"And this is the tale that I shall tell: To them I shall say that as I sat under this shelter skinning my dead cow, there appeared suddenly two men who fell upon me without warning; that in the struggle they hurt my poor leg most grievously, then, having choked me into quietude, they tied my limbs, despoiled me of my provender and hurriedly departed, leaving me helpless. I shall describe these two brutal men—oh, most minutely I shall describe them. And my description will be accurate, for you I shall be describing as you stand now; myself I shall describe as I now am.

"The man from the train will say: 'Yes, yes, that is true; those are surely the two I saw.' He will believe me at once. Then they will inquire to know in which direction fled this pair of scoundrels and I will tell them they went that way yonder to the south across the desert, and they will set off in that direction, seeking two who flee together, when all the while you will be gone north into those mountains which will shelter you. And that, Señor, will be a rich part of the whole joke.

"Perhaps, though, they question me further. Then I say: 'Take me before this gringo who within a week hired me to watch his sheep. Confront me with him. He will identify me, he will confirm my story.' And if they do that and he does that—as most surely he will—why, then they must turn me loose and that, Señor, will be the very crown and peak of the joke.'"

In the excess of his admiration and his gratitude, the Italian just naturally had to kiss him again.

They worked fast and they worked scientifically, carefully, overlooking nothing, providing against every contingency. But at the last minute, when the Italian was ready to resume his flight and the Spaniard, smoothly shaven and effectually disguised in the soiled shirt and messy overalls of the dead man, had turned around and submitted his wrists to be pinioned, it was discovered that there was no rope available with which to bind his legs. The one short scrap of rope about the spot had been used for tying his hands.

The Spaniard said this was just as well. Any binding that was drawn snugly enough to fetter his feet securely would certainly increase the pain in the inflamed and grossly swollen ankle joint.

However, it was apparent that he must be securely anchored, lest suspicion arise in the minds of his rescuers when they arrived. Here the Italian made a contribution to the plot. He was proud of his inspiration.

With the Mexican's butcher knife he cut long narrow strips from the fresh slick cowhide. Then the Spaniard sat down on the earth with his back against one of the slim tree trunks supporting the arbor, and the Italian took numerous turns about his waist and his arms and the upper part of his body, and tightly knotted the various ends of the skin ribbons behind the post. Unaided, no human being could escape out of that mesh. To the pressure of the prisoner's trunk, the moist pliant lashings would give slightly but it was certain they neither would work loose nor snap apart.

So he settled himself in his bonds, and the Italian, having shouldered his pack, once more fervently kissed his benefactor in token of gratitude, wished him success and made off with many farewells.

So far as this empty country was concerned, the Italian was a greenhorn, a tenderfoot. Nevertheless, he made excellent progress. He marched northward until dark, lay that night under a murdered man's smelly blanket behind a many-colored butte and next morning struck deeper into the broken lands. He entered what he hoped might be a gap through the mountains, treading cautiously along a narrow natural trail halfway up a dauntingly steep cliff side.

He was well into it when his foot dislodged a scrap of shaly rock which in sliding over the verge set other rocks to cascading down the slope. From above, yet larger boulders began toppling over into the scoured-out passageway thus provided, and during the next five minutes the walled-in declivity was alive and roaring with tumbling huge stones, with dislodged earth running fluid like a stream, with uprooted stunty piñons, with choking acrid dust clouds.

The Italian ran for dear life; he managed to get out of the avalanche's path. When at length he reached a safe place and looked back, he saw behind him how the landslide had choked the gorge almost to its brim. No human being—no, not even a goat, could from his side scale that jagged and overhanging parapet. Between him and pursuit was a perfect barrier.

Well content, he went on. But presently he made a discovery, a distressing discovery which took the good cheer right out of him. This was no gateway into which he had entered. It was a dead end leading nowhere— what Westerners call a box canyon. On three sides of him, right, left and on ahead, rose tremendously high walls, sheer and unclimbable. They threatened him; they seemed to be closing in on him to pinch him flat. And, of course, back of him retreat was cut off. There he was, bottled up like a fly in a corked jug, like a frog at the bottom of a well.

Frantically he explored as best he could the confines

of this vast prison cell of his. He stumbled upon a spring, and its waters, while tainted lightly with alkali, were drinkable. So he had water and he had food, some food. By paring his daily portions down almost to starvation point, he might make these rations last for months. But then, what? And in the meantime, what? Why, until hunger destroyed him, he was faced with that doom which he so dreaded—the doom of solitary confinement.

He thought it all out and then he knelt down and took out his pistol and he killed himself.

In one of his calculations that smart malefactor, the Spaniard, had been wrong. By his system of deductions, the searchers should reach the 'dobe hut where he was tethered within four hours or, at most, five. But it was nearer thirty hours before they appeared.

The trouble had been that the brakeman wasn't quite sure of the particular stretch where he had seen the fugitives nestled beneath a reaping machine on that flat car. Besides, it took time to spread the word; to summon county officials; to organize an armed searching party. When at length the posse did strike the five-mile trail leading from the railroad tracks to the camp of the late sheep herder, considerably more than a day had elapsed.

The track was fairly plain—two sets of heavy footprints bearing north and only lacking where rocky outcrops broke through the surface of the desert. Having found it, they followed it fast, and when they mounted the fold in the earth above the cabin, they saw the figure of a man seated in front of it, bound snugly to one of the supports of the arbor.

Hurrying toward him they saw that he was dead—that his face was blackened and horribly distorted; that his glazed eyes goggled at them and his tongue protruded; that his stiffened legs were drawn up in sharp angles of agony.

They looked closer and they saw the manner of his death and were very sorry for him. He had been bound with strands of fresh rawhide, and all through that day he had been sitting there exposed to the baking heat of the day.

Now heat, operating on damp new rawhide, has an immediate effect. Heat causes certain substances to expand but green rawhide it causes to contract very fast to an ironlike stiffness and rigidity.

So in this case the sun glare had drawn tighter and tighter the lashings about this poor devil's body, squeezing him in at the stomach and the breast and the shoulders, pressing his arms tighter and tighter and yet tighter against his sides. That for him would have been a highly unpleasant procedure but it would not have killed him.

Something else had done that. One loop of the rawhide had been twisted about his neck and made fast at the back of the post. At first it might have been no more than a loosely fitting circlet but hour by hour it had shrunk into a choking collar, a diminishing noose, a terrible deadly yoke. Veritably it had garroted him by inches.

Mrs. Manifold
by STEPHEN GRENDON

I don't know whether I would have gone into the *Sailors' Rest* if I had seen its proprietress before I saw the grimy card with its scrawled "Clerk Wanted" in the window. But perhaps I would—a man with less than a shilling in his pocket, and little chance to add to that, can't hesitate too much. Still, there was something about Mrs. Manifold, something you could feel but hardly put into words. I never saw anyone so fat; though she was a short woman, she weighed over three hundred

pounds, and it was easy to understand why she pre-
ferred to keep to her own room on the fourth floor—a
gable room.

"Ever been a clerk before, Mr. Robinson?" she asked
me.

Her voice was thin, high almost piping; it was a small
voice for so big a woman, and because it was so shrill and
penetrating, the contrast was the more startling.

"No. But I can read and write; I can add figures, if it
comes to that," I said.

She gave me a sharp glance. "It's plain to see you've
had some schooling. Down on your luck, is it?"

I admitted that.

She sat looking at me, humming a queer little tune,
which I came to recognize later when she sang it: a sea-
chanty. In all that tremendous bulk, only her eyes
seemed to move: small, black, with soot-lashed eyelids;
there was no evidence that she breathed, no tremor
disturbed her flesh, clad in a dress of black satin, which
despite her great mass, was frilled and ruffled like a
child's frock. Her eyes scrutinized me with a kind of bold
furtiveness, her fat fingers resting on the arms of the
chair which contained her strangely motionless body.
There was something horrible, not in a bestial sense, but
in a spiritual way, about her—not in any one facet, but
in everything—something that suggested terror.

"My clientele," she said in a voice suddenly subdued,
but with a crafty smile, "might not always be a nice one,
Mr. Robinson. A rough lot, Mr. Robinson. You wouldn't
expect anything else of Wapping, now, would you? Or
of somebody like Mrs. Ambrose Manifold?"

Then she tittered. A faint ripple disturbed that vast bulk, and the effect was wholly horrible.

"I can hold my own," I said.

"Perhaps. Perhaps. We shall see, Mr. Robinson. Your duties will be simple. You know what an innkeeper's clerk must do. Make them sign the register, Mr. Robinson. Sometimes they have reason to avoid it. Once a week, you will bring the register up to me. I wish to examine it. The money will be deposited to my account at the Bridsley Bank whenever and as soon as it collects to fifty pounds. I am not at home to anyone. Begin now."

Thereupon she rang a little bell, and the old man who had conducted me up the stairs led the way back down, having been instructed by Mrs. Manifold that I was to begin my duties at once.

I lost no time acquainting myself with my surroundings. While the old man, whose name was Mr. Claitor, removed the sign from the window and put it carefully away, with an air of doubtless needing it soon again, I took a look at the registry. It was nothing but an old ledger, on the first page of which someone had written in a flowing hand, *"Sailors' Rest*—Registry." There were two floors of rooms, which someone's fancy had numbered, to make seven in all—four on the second, three on the third; the first floor being given over to the kitchen, the small lobby, and three closet-like rooms for the staff. One of these was occupied by Mr. Claitor, another by Mr. and Mrs. Jeffers, and the third by the clerk of *Sailors' Rest*. Six of the rooms were occupied at four shillings the night, six for day and night; evidently there were no rates by the week. The lobby had an appearance of genteel shabbiness; it was not exactly dirty, but it was certainly not clean, and it conveyed the impression of never having been quite clean within the memory of any living person. The glass in the window and the door facing the street was fly-specked and dust-streaked, and there was about the entire building a faint but unmistakable odor of the river. The Thames flowed not far away, and at night its musk, rising with the fog, enclosed and permeated the old building.

Mr. Claitor, who was tall, thin, and grey, with the lugubrious expression of a very tired Great Dane, got around to instructing me, finally, that the lobby was to be closed promptly at nine o'clock every night, though, thereafter, I might expect to be summoned to open the door for one or more of our tenants come roistering home.

Probably there is nothing so tiring as the position as clerk in a shabby, hole-in-a-corner inn, which seems designed to attract only the dregs of mankind: the bitter, disillusioned old men of the sea—the hopeless wanderers haunting Limehouse and Whitechapel and Wapping—the hunted and the haunted and the lost. Yet, I suppose everyone in a position not especially to his liking is similarly convinced; the human being is essentially weak and insecure, no matter what his place in life, and if that place is not felicitous, that weakness makes itself manifest in dissatisfaction, out of which grows the conviction that anything at all is better than the present position. Work at the *Sailor's Rest* was monotonous, even when there were books to be read—which was not often, and it soon became a pattern.

But the weekly trip to Mrs. Manifold's gable room was somehow never quite part of that pattern. There was something a little different every time, despite the fact that her position never seemed to have changed; for all her appearance, she need never have moved from one week to the next, and not at all since first I saw her. Every time she would take the registry and examine the new entries.

"Roald Jensen," she read out slowly. "Now, what is he like? Is he a tall man or is he short?"

"Tall, thin, sandy-red hair, one wooden leg. He wears a moustache. Last sailed on the *Lofoten* out of Oslo."

"Frederick Schwartz, then. What is he like?"

"Short, fat. Looks like a German *burgomeister*. Red cheeks, blue eyes. Very talkative. Heavy German accent. Last sailed on the *Stresemann* out of Hamburg."

"Good gracious, Mr. Robinson," she said on occasion, "you should have been a policeman. I admire the quality of observation."

But, each time she said it, I caught the unmistakable impression that she was laughing at me behind her small, dark eyes; and each time she finished her examination of the registry, I could not escape the conviction that she did so with relief, so that I wondered often why she insisted on taking this trouble at all if she concluded it always with such manifest satisfaction at being done with it.

Once, she was talkative. She said comparatively little, but I learned from her that she had had some kind of place in Singapore half a dozen years ago or thereabouts; she and her husband had run it. Then she had come to England.

"And where is Mr. Manifold now?" I asked her.

"Ah, nobody knows, nobody knows. Nobody, Mr. Robinson."

Thereafter she had given the unmistakable sign of having finished with me—closing her eyes and leaning back, inert, save for a trembling of her thick lips, as she hummed the chanty she sometimes sang.

> *Oh, the Captain's in the brig, Lads,*
> *The First Mate's brains are blown;*
> *We'll sail the Seven Seas, Lads,*
> *And make them all our own . . .*

But there were diversions, though they were out of the ordinary.

Sometimes gentlemen from the C. I. D. at Scotland Yard came around to look for somebody—on the average, once a fortnight. Sometimes one of our registrants walked out and never came back, leaving all his baggage behind to be stored against his return—which might not happen. Things could happen in the fog; things could take place no one ever found out—robbery and sudden death, suicide sometimes. I never felt any inclination to go outside on a foggy night; daytime was dreary enough, for the *Sailors' Rest* was not in a good neighborhood—oh, good enough for what it was, I suppose, but not good enough for what it might have been. And there was something about Mrs. Manifold, too, that seemed to say she had known better days and a better business than this, even if in Singapore.

Singapore! Perhaps it had its holes like *Sailors' Rest,* its districts like Wapping, too—but, being far away, it was caught in a kind of magic aura, it took on color and life and drama built up solely in imagination, as of all faraway places which are never, somehow, quite real, and always, always wonderfully exciting. Why had Mrs. Manifold left Singapore to come to London? And why had she come down into Wapping, of all places? But here she was, and apparently content to be here, making no complaint, occasionally even making sly remarks about her reduced station in life. Yet she need not have been here, for her balance at the bank was always written in five figures—in ready funds alone, she was worth more than fifty thousand pounds.

But for all the signs of breeding which showed through, there was never anything which could dispel that feeling of terror she could induce. Did it arise out of her shocking obesity, or from some other, hidden source? All too often revulsion stimulates dislike and hatred; it is impossible sometimes to uncover the roots of fear or horror. Curiously, she had but one taboo, about which I heard from Mr. Claitor, when he came to my room one night.

"Mrs. Manifold says you are not to drink wine, Mr. Robinson. No wine in the house, she says. It's the rule of *Sailors' Rest.*"

When I mentioned it to her, she confirmed it. "Wine I cannot abide, Mr. Robinson. Ale, yes. Vermouth, certainly. Whatever you wish—but no wine."

She occupied her gable in lordly splendor. Splendor

being relative, her self-denial did not diminish it. She ruled *Sailors' Rest* with an unchallenged and indomitable will. In a sense, she was *Sailors' Rest,* and *Sailors' Rest* was Mrs. Manifold; sometimes at night, in that borderland between sleep and waking, I thought of the old building as somehow alive. I thought of the wide, fly-specked, dust-streaked window in front expanding briefly, fleetingly into a sly-lipped smile, something akin to a leer. Like the fog and the musk of the Thames, Mrs. Manifold's presence permeated the very walls, made itself felt in every nook and cranny, and lingered in the quiet air.

In the middle of my eleventh week, early one hot summer night, there came an old sailor just in on *H. M. S. Malaya,* out of Singapore. A Yankee, by the look of him, with a brush of short beard reaching around his chin from one ear to another: a Quaker cut, I think they call it. He was in his sixties, I judged, and did not like the look of the place, saying so, and adding that there was no other.

"I'll stay the night," he said.

"American?" I asked.

"Born there. Spent most of my life in Singapore."

Perhaps it was natural that I should ask whether he had ever heard of Mrs. Ambrose Manifold. There was nothing to show that he was within shouting distance of her.

"Mrs. Manifold," he said, and grinned. "Mister, there was a woman. Big enough for half a dozen women."

"Why did she leave Singapore?"

"Who knows? Women don't do things sensible, Mister. Amby run out on her, and off she went. Biggest thing I ever seen to drop out of sight like that!"

"What happened to him?" I asked.

"Nobody knows that, Mister. They didn't get along too well sometimes. Amby liked to drink—he was a wine drinker. He could get stewed on wine faster'n you could say Jack Robinson. Your name ain't Jack, is it?"

"No," I said. "It doesn't matter."

"Well, Amby run out on her, though how he did it, God knows. And he took along the biggest cask of wine they had in the cellar. The way she watched him and all, he was sly and fast to get out—and with that wine, too! Nobody ever saw him go—but the cask of wine he had hauled out bold as brass! He had his mind made up, Mister—and so would you, if you ever saw Mrs. Manifold. What could a man do with a woman as fat as that, eh, Mister?"

He poked me in the ribs and said that he was tired.

In the morning he was gone, but he had paid in advance; so it was his privilege to go when he liked. It was necessary to get a one-night payment in advance to guard against this method of departure.

And that weekend, when Mrs. Manifold came upon his name, her eyes held to it, and she began to tremble —a strange sight, like the shaking of jelly, a shuddering and trembling that was unpleasant to behold.

"Joshua Bennington. Mr. Robinson—a well-built man with a brown beard, was he? From Singapore. One night, too! In mid-week. Ah, too bad, too bad! Why didn't you let me know?"

"I had no idea you would want to know before now. I have my instructions."

"Yes, yes—that's true. Singapore! I would have liked to talk to him."

She said no more, but there was a strange expression in her eyes. I could not fathom it. Triumph, amusement, regret—all these were there—or were they only reflections from my own imagination? It was difficult to tell with Mrs. Manifold. But the trembling in her body continued for a long time, and I was anxious to get away, to get out of that gable room, to escape the burden of her eyes.

Three days after that, something changed in that old inn.

The change was in Mrs. Manifold, too, and it happened after the empty seventh room was filled. He came in just before closing time, a small man with a limp, with his hat pulled down low, and his face all muffled up against the fog which was so thick it had got into the lobby and was yellow in the light at the desk. He was wet with it, wet with fog—and inside wet—with wine. For he reeked of it—stronger than the room reeked of the fog and the river's smell; the sickish smell of sweet wine hung about him like a cloud.

A strange man and a silent one.

"Good evening, sir," I said.

No answer.

I turned the registry toward him, holding out the pen.

"Number seven left, sir," I said. "Will it be for the night or longer?"

What he said sounded like, "Longer," but his voice was so muffled I could not easily tell.

"A wet night, sir," I said.

He signed the registry in a crabbed hand, writing with difficulty, and without removing his tattered gloves.

"Third floor back, last door. It's standing open," I said.

Without a word he left the lobby for the stairs, trailing that nauseating smell of wine.

I looked at the registry.

The writing was difficult, but it could be read, after a fashion. Unless the fog and the addling sweetness of the wine-smell and my imagination deceived me, I read there, "Amb. Manifold, late of Singapore, out of Madeira."

I took the registry and mounted to the fourth floor. The crack under the door showed a light. I knocked.

"It's Robinson, Mrs. Manifold," I said. "You told me if we ever got anybody else from Singapore . . ."

"Come in."

I went in. She was still sitting there in her black satin dress, like a queen in the middle of the room.

"Let me see," she said eagerly.

I put the registry before her.

And then she saw. Her dark-skinned face went pale, and if she had trembled before, she shook now—a great shaking animating that mass of flesh. She pushed the book away, and it fell to the floor. I bent and picked it up.

"Seems to be the same name as your own," I said.

With some effort at control, she asked the familiar question. "What is he like?"

"Short—a small man—with a limp."

"Where is he?"

"In number seven—just under you."

"I want to see him."

"Now?"

"Now, Mr. Robinson."

I went down the stairs and knocked on the door of number seven. No answer. I knocked louder. Still no answer. A surly, unpleasant man, certainly. I knocked once more. Still no answer.

I tried the door. It was open.

I pushed it ajar and said softly into the darkness, "Mr. Manifold?"

No answer.

I opened the door all the way and turned up the light.

The room was empty. Empty, that is, of human occupation—it was alive with the rich headiness of wine, a sickening sweetness, cloying and repelling. There was no sign that the bed had been touched; yet the door of the room was closed, where it had been open before; so he had been there, since no one else had.

I went downstairs into the lobby, but no one was there, and the outer door was locked, as I had left it. Mr. Manifold was nowhere to be seen.

I went back to the gable room where Mrs. Manifold waited.

"Well?" she asked, seeing me alone.

"I can't find him," I said. "I tried his room, but he's gone."

She was still shaking, but in the midst of her inner turmoil, she asked, "Mr. Robinson, have you been drinking wine?"

"No. That smell came in with him. He's been drinking, I suspect. Madeira, I think—or something equally heavy. A sweet port . . ."

But she was not listening. Or rather, she was not listening to me. Her little eyes had narrowed, and she was leaning a little to one side, with her massive head on her great shoulders cocked somewhat to the left and down, as if she were listening to something from below.

"Do you hear someone singing, Mr. Robinson?" she asked in a harsh whisper.

"Can't say as I do," I answered, after a moment of listening.

"It goes like this," she said, and sang with horrible urgency the familiar lines of her own chanty—

> *"Oh, the Captain's in the brig, Lads,*
> *The First Mate's brains are blown;*
> *We'll sail the Seven Seas, Lads,*
> *And make them all our own . . ."*

"No," I said.

She closed her eyes and leaned back. "Let me know when you see him again, Mr. Robinson."

After that, Mrs. Manifold's bell rang several times a day for me.

First it was, "Get that smell of wine out of this house, Mr. Robinson."

But I couldn't. Open doors and windows as I would, I couldn't get that smell of wine out: there it was—rich, heady, nauseating: it had come in to stay, and there was nothing to do but live with it. I could imagine how it bothered her, what with her hatred for the stuff, but it was in her room, too, and she had to endure it as well as the rest of us.

Then, afterward, it was about Mr. Manifold. Had I seen him?

No, I had not. I never saw him again. He had gone without paying, but then, he never rightly used that room except to put the smell of wine into it, and there was no charge for that.

And did I hear that singing?

I never did.

But she did, and it bothered her. And it bothered her, too, to hear Mr. Manifold the way she said she did. She knew his walk; there was a slight drag because of that limp. I never heard anything like that, and neither did anyone else, for she did ask Mr. Claitor, who had not even seen Mr. Manifold, as I had.

I used to ask myself, if he were indeed her husband, why had he come? And, having come, why had he gone without so much as saying hello or good-by to his wife? It was strange—but *Sailors' Rest* was a place for strange things to happen even in the ordinary course of its monotonous existence.

Mrs. Manifold was not the same.

If anything, she was more terrible. There was a greater furtiveness about her; there was less sly humor, almost nothing of humor at all; there was an unmistakable grimness, a kind of terrible bravado; and there was above everything else something about her that made her far more horrible than she had ever seemed to me— something that made me think of death and fear of death, of violence and unimaginable horror, something that throbbed in the core of Mrs. Manifold as the red blood coursed through the heart keeping life in that bulging mound of flesh.

And being with her even for the little whiles I had to be there was infinitely unpleasant, for she was always listening, catching her breath and listening, and hearing things when there was nothing to hear. And she was always asking questions I couldn't answer to please her, and scolding at me to clear the air of that wine smell, which was impossible—but I needn't ever have told her for all the impression it made on her. And she went on, sometimes, about her husband.

"Always the wine and never tending to business, that was Ambrose," she said. "I gave him wine—more than he could drink, curse his black soul!"

I heard that over and over. If I heard it once, I heard it a score of times. It was better than that terrible listening. You can't imagine what it is until you go through such a thing by yourself. Even today, long after my short tenure at *Sailors' Rest,* I can see that horrible, obese woman with her flesh lapping out over the sides of her chair, pushing out between the slats, leaning that vast bulk over to listen with her black-haired head and the golden hooped earrings glistening in the feeble yellow light that was in the room, to listen for the sound of singing and the dragging limp; I can still hear her shrill, piping voice complain about the stench of wine, the nauseating sweetness of that cloying odor brought into the *Sailors' Rest* on that fateful night of fog.

And then, one night, the end came.

I woke out of my sleep, and that wine-smell was thick enough to choke me. I got up and opened the door of my room, and then I heard the singing—something like she said, only a little different, and it went like this—

> *"Oh, the Old Man's in the Deep, Lads,*
> *The Madam's packed and flown—*
> *I'll sail the Seven Seas, Lads,*
> *Until I find her home . . ."*

It was coming from somewhere upstairs; so I went back and put something on. I came out again and started up the stairs, and I thought I could hear that dragging walk Mrs. Manifold always said she heard, but I could not be sure.

I got up to the third flight of stairs when I heard her scream. It was Mrs. Manifold's voice, shrill and awful, and she was screaming at her husband.

"Go away, Ambrose! Go back!" she cried in that horrible, piping voice that came so unnaturally from her obese body. "Don't touch me!"

And then there was just a terrible, unnatural scream, diminishing into a choking, gurgling sound.

I was struck motionless with fright until Claitor came up behind me, agitated and scared; then I pulled myself together and ran up to the fourth floor. Claitor was right behind me, which turned out to be the best thing for me, since he could testify later on, and there was nothing the people at Scotland Yard could do to me.

Because Mrs. Manifold was dead—choked to death. She lay there on the floor, with her black satin dress ripped down one side, and her white flesh pushing out from the tear, and her eyes turned up. All over the room there was a smell of sweet wine so thick that it seemed there was no air left—only that sickening smell.

And there was something else—something that shouldn't have been, something nobody could explain.

There were bones scattered in the room, human bones, a man's bones—and sharp, deep marks in Mrs. Manifold's neck where she had been choked, and pieces of cloth and a battered old hat I had seen once before on a night when the fog was yellow in the light at the desk of the *Sailors' Rest* . . .

There was nothing Scotland Yard could say to explain all that.

But then, there was no reason why they should think of any connection between what happened up there in that gable room where Mrs. Manifold was hiding and what they found up the Thames from its mouth, far up, in Wapping. An old wine cask out of Singapore, a cask that had once held Madeira and now was stove in at one end, and held nothing but the bones of two toes and a finger—nothing to tell them that Mrs. Manifold had killed her husband and put his body in that cask of wine and had it carried far out to sea, weighted perhaps, to sink until time and the tide carried it far from

Singapore—just as whatever it was came into the *Sailors' Rest* that foggy night and put it down in the registry—

"Amb. Manifold, late of Singapore, out of Madeira."

Or was it somebody's ghoulish sense of humor? Out of Madeira indeed! I cannot abide the smell of it to this day!

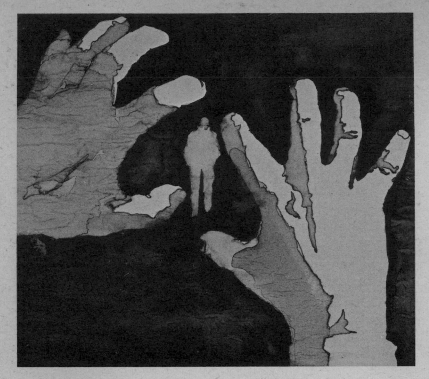

The Hands of Mr. Ottermole
by THOMAS BURKE

At six o'clock of a January evening Mr. Whybrow was walking home through the cobweb alleys of London's East End. He had left the golden clamor of the great High Street to which the tram had brought him from the river and his daily work, and was now in the chessboard of byways that is called Mallon End. None of the rush and gleam of the High Street trickled into these byways. A few paces south—a flood tide of life, foaming and beating. Here—only slow-shuffling figures and muffled pulses. He was in the sink of London, the last refuge of European vagrants.

As though in tune with the street's spirit, he too walked slowly, with head down. It seemed that he was pondering some pressing trouble, but he was not. He had no trouble. He was walking slowly because he had been on his feet all day, and he was bent in abstraction because he was wondering whether the Missis would have herrings for his tea, or haddock; and he was trying to decide which would be the more tasty on a night like this. A wretched night it was, of damp and mist, and the mist wandered into his throat and his eyes, and the damp had settled on pavement and roadway, and where the sparse lamplight fell it sent up a greasy sparkle that chilled one to look at. By contrast it made his speculations more agreeable, and made him ready for that tea— whether herring or haddock. His eye turned from the glum bricks that made his horizon, and went forward half a mile. He saw a gas-lit kitchen, a flamy fire and a spread tea table. There was toast in the hearth and a singing kettle on the side and a piquant effusion of herrings, or maybe of haddock, or perhaps sausages. The vision gave his aching feet a throb of energy. He shook imperceptible damp from his shoulders, and hastened towards its reality.

But Mr. Whybrow wasn't going to get any tea that evening—or any other evening. Mr. Whybrow was going to die. Somewhere within a hundred yards of him another man was walking: a man much like Mr. Whybrow and much like any other man, but without the only quality that enables mankind to live peaceably together and not as madmen in a jungle. A man with a dead heart eating into itself and bringing forth the foul organisms that arise from death and corruption. And that thing in man's shape, on a whim or a settled idea—one cannot know—had said within himself that Mr. Whybrow should never taste another herring. Not that Mr. Whybrow had injured him. Not that he had any dislike of Mr. Whybrow. Indeed, he knew nothing of him save as a familiar figure about the streets. But, moved by a force that had taken possession of his empty cells, he had picked on Mr. Whybrow with that blind choice that makes us pick one restaurant table that has nothing to mark it from four or five other tables, or one apple from a dish of half a dozen equal apples; or that drives Nature to send a cyclone upon one corner of this planet, and destroy five hundred lives in that corner, and leave another five hundred in the same corner unharmed. So this man had picked on Mr. Whybrow, as he might have picked on you or me, had we been within his daily observation; and even now he was creeping through the blue-toned streets, nursing his large white hands, moving ever closer to Mr. Whybrow's tea table, and so closer to Mr. Whybrow himself.

He wasn't, this man, a bad man. Indeed, he had many of the social and amiable qualities, and passed as a respectable man, as most successful criminals do. But the thought had come into his moldering mind that he would like to murder somebody, and, as he held no fear of God or man, he was going to do it, and would then go home to *his* tea. I don't say that flippantly, but as a statement of fact. Strange as it may seem to the humane, murderers must and do sit down to meals after a murder. There is no reason why they shouldn't, and many reasons why they should. For one thing, they need to keep their physical and mental vitality at full beat for the business of covering their crime. For another, the strain of their effort makes them hungry, and satisfaction at the accomplishment of a desired thing brings a feeling of relaxation towards human pleasures. It is accepted among non-murderers that the murderer is always overcome by fear for his safety and horror at his act; but this type is rare. His own safety is, of course, his immediate concern, but vanity is a marked quality of most murderers, and that, together with the thrill of conquest, makes him confident that he can secure it, and when he has restored his strength with food he goes about securing it as a young hostess goes about the arranging of her first big dinner—a little anxious, but no more. Criminologists and detectives tell us that *every* murderer, however intelligent or cunning, always makes one slip in his tactics—one little slip that brings the affair home to him. But that is only half true. It is true only of the murderers who are caught. Scores of murderers are not caught: therefore scores of murderers do not make any mistake at all. This man didn't.

As for horror or remorse, prison chaplains, doctors and lawyers have told us that of murderers they have interviewed under condemnation and the shadow of death, only one here and there has expressed any contrition for his act, or shown any sign of mental misery. Most of them display only exasperation at having been caught when so many have gone undiscovered, or indig-

nation at being condemned for a perfectly reasonable
act. However normal and humane they may have been
before the murder, they are utterly without conscience
after it. For what is conscience? Simply a polite nickname for superstition, which is a polite nickname for
fear. Those who associate remorse with murder are, no
doubt, basing their ideas on the world legend of the
remorse of Cain, or are projecting their own frail minds
into the mind of the murderer, and getting false reac-
tions. Peaceable folk cannot hope to make contact with
this mind, for they are not merely different in mental
type from the murderer: they are different in their per-
sonal chemistry and construction. Some men can and
do kill, not one man, but two or three, and go calmly
about their daily affairs. Other men could not, under
the most agonizing provocation, bring themselves even
to wound. It is men of this sort who imagine the murderer in torments of remorse and fear of the law,
whereas he is actually sitting down to his tea.

The man with the large white hands was as ready for
his tea as Mr. Whybrow was, but he had something to
do before he went to it. When he had done that something, and made no mistake about it, he would be even
more ready for it, and would go to it as comfortably as
he went to it the day before, when his hands were stain-
less.

Walk on, then, Mr. Whybrow, walk on; and as you
walk, look your last upon the familiar features of your
nightly journey. Follow your jack-o'-lantern tea table.
Look well upon its warmth and color and kindness; feed
your eyes with it, and tease your nose with its gentle

domestic odors; for you will never sit down to it. Within ten minutes' pacing of you a pursuing phantom has spoken in his heart, and you are doomed. There you go —you and phantom—two nebulous dabs of mortality, moving through green air along pavements of powder blue, the one to kill, the other to be killed. Walk on. Don't annoy your burning feet by hurrying, for the more slowly you walk, the longer you will breathe the green air of this January dusk, and see the dreamy lamp-light and the little shops, and hear the agreeable commerce of the London crowd and the haunting pathos of the street organ. These things are dear to you, Mr. Whybrow. You don't know it now, but in fifteen minutes you will have two seconds in which to realize how inexpressibly dear they are.

Walk on, then, across this crazy chessboard. You are in Lagos Street now, among the tents of the wanderers of Eastern Europe. A minute or so, and you are in Loyal Lane, among the lodging houses that shelter the useless and the beaten of London's camp followers. The lane holds the smell of them, and its soft darkness seems heavy with the wail of the futile. But you are not sensitive to impalpable things, and you plod through it, unseeing, as you do every evening, and come to Blean Street, and plod through that. From basement to sky rise the tenements of an alien colony. Their windows slot the ebony of their walls with lemon. Behind those windows strange life is moving, dressed with forms that are not of London or of England, yet, in essence, the same agreeable life that you have been living, and to-night will live no more. From high above you comes a

voice crooning *The Song of Katta.* Through a window
you see a family keeping a religious rite. Through another you see a woman pouring out tea for her husband.
You see a man mending a pair of boots; a mother bathing her baby. You have seen all these things before, and
never noticed them. You do not notice them now, but if
you knew that you were never going to see them again,
you would notice them. You never *will* see them again,
not because your life has run its natural course, but
because a man whom you have often passed in the street
has at his own solitary pleasure decided to usurp the
awful authority of nature, and destroy you. So perhaps
it's as well that you don't notice them, for your part in
them is ended. No more for you these pretty moments
of our earthly travail: only one moment of terror, and
then a plunging darkness.

Closer to you this shadow of massacre moves, and
now he is twenty yards behind you. You can hear his
footfall, but you do not turn your head. You are familiar
with footfalls. You are in London, in the easy security
of your daily territory, and footfalls behind you, your
instinct tells you, are no more than a message of human
company.

But can't you hear something in those footfalls—
something that goes with a widdershins beat? Something that says: *Look out, look out. Beware, beware.*
Can't you hear the very syllables of *mur-der-er, mur-
der-er?* No; there is nothing in footfalls. They are neu-
tral. The foot of villainy falls with the same quiet note
as the foot of honesty. But those footfalls, Mr. Whybrow, are bearing on to you a pair of hands, and there

is something in hands. Behind you that pair of hands is even now stretching its muscles in preparation for your end. Every minute of your days you have been seeing human hands. Have you ever realized the sheer horror of hands—those appendages that are a symbol for our moments of trust and affection and salutation? Have you thought of the sickening potentialities that lie within the scope of that five-tentacled member? No, you never have; for all the human hands that you have seen have been stretched to you in kindness or fellowship. Yet, though the eyes can hate, and the lips can sting, it is only that dangling member that can gather the accumulated essence of evil, and electrify it into currents of destruction. Satan may enter into man by many doors, but in the hands alone can he find the servants of his will.

Another minute, Mr. Whybrow, and you will know all about the horror of human hands.

You are nearly home now. You have turned into your street—Caspar Street—and you are in the center of the chessboard. You can see the front window of your little four-roomed house. The street is dark, and its three lamps give only a smut of light that is more confusing than darkness. It is dark—empty, too. Nobody about; no lights in the front parlors of the houses, for the families are at tea in their kitchens; and only a random glow in a few upper rooms occupied by lodgers. Nobody about but you and your following companion, and you don't notice him. You see him so often that he is never seen. Even if you turned your head and saw him, you would only say "Good evening" to him, and walk on. A suggestion that he was a possible murderer would not even make you laugh. It would be too silly.

And now you are at your gate. And now you have found your door key. And now you are in, and hanging up your hat and coat. The Missis has just called a greeting from the kitchen, whose smell is an echo of that greeting (herrings!) and you have answered it, when the door shakes under a sharp knock.

Go away, Mr. Whybrow. Go away from that door. Don't touch it. Get right away from it. Get out of the house. Run with the Missis to the back garden, and over the fence. Or call the neighbors. But don't touch that door. Don't, Mr. Whybrow, don't open . . .

Mr. Whybrow opened the door.

That was the beginning of what became known as London's Strangling Horrors. Horrors they were called because they were something more than murders: they were motiveless, and there was an air of black magic about them. Each murder was committed at a time when the street where the bodies were found was empty of any perceptible or possible murderer. There would be an empty alley. There would be a policeman at its end. He would turn his back on the empty alley for less than a minute. Then he would look around and run into the night with news of another strangling. And in any direction he looked nobody to be seen and no report to be had of anybody being seen. Or he would be on duty in a long-quiet street, and suddenly be called to a house of dead people whom a few seconds earlier he had seen alive. And, again, whichever way he looked nobody to be seen; and although police whistles put an immediate cordon around the area, and searched all houses, no possible murderer to be found.

The first news of the murder of Mr. and Mrs. Whybrow was brought by the station sergeant. He had been walking through Caspar Street on his way to the station for duty, when he noticed the open door of No. 98. Glancing in, he saw by the gaslight of the passage a motionless body on the floor. After a second look he blew his whistle, and when the constables answered him he took one to join him in a search of the house, and sent others to watch all neighboring streets, and make inquiries at adjoining houses. But neither in the house nor in the streets was anything found to indicate the murderer. Neighbors on either side, and opposite, were questioned, but they had seen nobody about, and had heard nothing. One had heard Mr. Whybrow come home —the scrape of his latchkey in the door was so regular an evening sound, he said, that you could set your watch by it for half past six—but he had heard nothing more than the sound of the opening door until the sergeant's whistle. Nobody had been seen to enter the house or leave it, by front or back, and the necks of the dead people carried no fingerprints or other traces. A nephew was called in to go over the house, but he could find nothing missing; and anyway his uncle possessed nothing worth stealing. The little money in the house was untouched, and there were no signs of any disturbance of the property, or even of struggle. No signs of anything but brutal and wanton murder.

Mr. Whybrow was known to neighbors and workmates as a quiet, likeable, home-loving man; such a man as could not have any enemies. But, then, murdered men seldom have. A relentless enemy who hates a man to the point of wanting to hurt him seldom wants to murder him, since to do that puts him beyond suffering. So the police were left with an impossible situation: no clue to the murderer and no motive for the murders; only the fact that they had been done.

The first news of the affair sent a tremor through London generally, and an electric thrill through all Mallon End. Here was a murder of two inoffensive people, not for gain and not for revenge; and the murderer, to whom, apparently, killing was a casual impulse, was at large. He had left no traces, and, provided he had no companions, there seemed no reason why he should not remain at large. Any clear-headed man who stands alone, and has no fear of God or man, can, if he chooses, hold a city, even a nation, in subjection; but your every-day criminal is seldom clear-headed, and dislikes being lonely. He needs, if not the support of confederates, at least somebody to talk to; his vanity needs the satisfaction of perceiving at first hand the effect of his work. For this he will frequent bars and coffee shops and other public places. Then, sooner or later, in a glow of comradeship, he will utter the one word too much; and the nark, who is everywhere, has an easy job.

But though saloons and other places were "combed" and set with watches, and it was made known by whispers that good money and protection were assured to those with information, nothing attaching to the Whybrow case could be found. The murderer clearly had no friends and kept no company. Known men of this type were called up and questioned, but each was able to give a good account of himself; and in a few days the police were at a dead end. Against the constant public gibe that the thing had been done almost under their noses, they became restive, and for four days each man of the force was working his daily beat under a strain. On the fifth day they became still more restive.

It was the season of annual teas and entertainments for the children of the Sunday Schools, and on an evening of fog, when London was a world of groping phantoms, a small girl, in the bravery of best Sunday frock and shoes, shining face and new-washed hair, set out from Logan Passage for St. Michael's Parish Hall. She never got there. She was not actually dead until half past six, but she was as good as dead from the moment she left her mother's door. Somebody like a man, pacing the street from which the Passage led, saw her come out; and from that moment she was dead. Through the fog somebody's large white hands reached after her, and in fifteen minutes they were about her.

At half past six a whistle screamed trouble, and those answering it found the body of little Nellie Vrinoff in a warehouse entry in Minnow Street. The sergeant was first among them, and he posted his men to useful points, ordering them here and there in the tart tones of repressed rage, and berating the officer whose beat the street was. "I saw you, Magson, at the end of the lane. What were you up to there? You were there ten minutes before you turned." Magson began an explanation about keeping an eye on a suspicious-looking character at that end, but the sergeant cut him short: "You don't want to look for suspicious characters. You want to look for *murderers*. Messing about . . . and then this happens right where you ought to be. Now think what they'll say."

With the speed of ill news came the crowd, pale and perturbed; and on the story that the unknown monster had appeared again, and this time to a child, their faces streaked the fog with spots of hate and horror. But then came the ambulance and more police, and swiftly they broke up the crowd; and as it broke the sergeant's thought was thickened into words, and from all sides came low murmurs of "Right under their noses." Later inquiries showed that four people of the district, above suspicion, had passed that entry at intervals of seconds before the murder, and seen nothing and heard nothing. None of them had passed the child alive or seen her dead. None of them had seen anybody in the street except themselves. Again the police were left with no motive and with no clue.

And now the district, as you will remember, was given over, not to panic, for the London public never yields to that, but to apprehension and dismay. If these things were happening in their familiar streets, then anything might happen. Wherever people met—in the streets, the markets and the shops—they debated the one topic. Women took to bolting their windows and doors at the first fall of dusk. They kept their children closely under their eye. They did their shopping before dark, and watched anxiously, while pretending they weren't watching, for the return of their husbands from work.

Under the Cockney's semi-humorous resignation to disaster, they hid an hourly foreboding. By the whim of one man with a pair of hands the structure and tenor of their daily life were shaken, as they always can be shaken by any man contemptuous of humanity and fearless of its laws. They began to realize that the pillars that supported the peaceable society in which they lived were mere straws that anybody could snap; that laws were powerful only so long as they were obeyed; that the police were potent only so long as they were feared. By the power of his hands this one man had made a whole community do something new: he had made it think, and left it gasping at the obvious.

And then, while it was yet gasping under his first two strokes, he made his third. Conscious of the horror that his hands had created, and hungry as an actor who has once tasted the thrill of the multitude, he made fresh advertisement of his presence; and on Wednesday morning, three days after the murder of the child, the papers carried to the breakfast tables of England the story of a still more shocking outrage.

At 9:32 on Tuesday night a constable was on duty in Jarnigan Road, and at that time spoke to a fellow officer named Petersen at the top of Clemming Street. He had seen this officer walk down that street. He could swear that the street was empty at that time, except for a lame bootblack whom he knew by sight, and who passed him and entered a tenement on the side opposite that on which his fellow officer was walking. He had the habit, as all constables had just then, of looking constantly behind him and around him, whichever way he was walking, and he was certain that the street was empty. He passed his sergeant at 9:33, saluted him, and answered his inquiry for anything seen. He reported that he had seen nothing and passed on. His beat ended at a short distance from Clemming Street, and, having paced it, he turned and came again at 9:34 to the top of the street. He had scarcely reached it before he heard the hoarse voice of the sergeant: "Gregory! You there? Quick. Here's another. My God, it's Petersen! Garotted. Quick, call 'em up!"

That was the third of the Strangling Horrors, of which there were to be a fourth and a fifth; and the five horrors were to pass into the unknown and unknowable. That is, unknown as far as authority and the public were concerned. The identity of the murderer *was* known, but to two men only. One was the murderer himself; the other was a young journalist.

This young man, who was covering the affairs for his paper, the *Daily Torch,* was no smarter than the other zealous newspaper men who were hanging about these byways in the hope of a sudden story. But he was patient, and he hung a little closer to the case than the other fellows, and by continually staring at it he at last raised the figure of the murderer like a genie from the stones on which he had stood to do his murders.

After the first few days the men had given up any attempt at exclusive stories, for there were none to be had. They met regularly at the police station, and what little information there was they shared. The officials were agreeable to them, but no more. The sergeant discussed with them the details of each murder; suggested possible explanations of the man's methods; recalled from the past those cases that had some similarity; and hinted that work was being done which would soon bring the business to an end; but about that work he would not say a word. The Inspector, too, was gracefully garrulous on the thesis of Murder, but whenever one of the party edged the talk towards what was being done in this immediate matter, he glided past it. Whatever the officials knew, they were not giving it to newspaper men. The business had fallen heavily upon them, and only by a capture made by their own efforts could they rehabilitate themselves in official and public esteem. Scotland Yard, of course, was at work, and had all the station's material; but the station's hope was that they themselves would have the honor of settling the affair; and however useful the coöperation of the Press might be in other cases, they did not want to risk a defeat by a premature disclosure of their theories and plans.

So the sergeant talked at large, and propounded one interesting theory after another, all of which the newspaper men had thought of themselves.

The young man soon gave up these morning lectures on the Philosophy of Crime, and took to wandering about the streets and making bright stories out of the effect of the murders on the normal life of the people. A melancholy job made more melancholy by the district. The littered roadways, the crestfallen houses, the bleared windows—all held the acid misery that evokes no sympathy: the misery of the frustrated poet. The misery was the creation of the aliens, who were living in this makeshift fashion because they had no settled homes, and would neither take the trouble to make a home where they *could* settle, nor get on with their wandering.

There was little to be picked up. All he saw and heard were indignant faces, and wild conjectures of the murderer's identity and of the secret of his trick of appearing and disappearing unseen. Since a policeman himself had fallen a victim, denunciations of the force had ceased, and the unknown was now invested with a cloak of legend. Men eyed other men, as though thinking: It might be *him*. It might be *him*. They were no longer looking for a man who had the air of a Madame Tussaud murderer; they were looking for a man, or perhaps some harridan woman, who had done these particular murders. Their thoughts ran mainly on the foreign set. Such ruffianism could scarcely belong to England, nor could the bewildering cleverness of the thing. So they turned to Roumanian gypsies and Turkish carpet sellers. There, clearly, would be found the "warm" spot. These Eastern fellows—they knew all sorts of tricks, and they had no real religion—nothing to hold them within bounds. Sailors returning from those parts had told tales of conjurors who made themselves invisible; and there were tales of Egyptian and Arab potions that were used for abysmally queer purposes. Perhaps it *was* possible to them; you never knew. They were so slick and cunning, and they had such gliding movements; no Englishman could melt away as they could. Almost certainly the murderer would be found to be one of that sort—with some dark trick of his own—and just because they were sure that he *was* a magician, they felt that it was useless to look for him. He was a power, able to hold them in subjection and to hold himself untouchable. Superstition, which so easily cracks the frail shell of reason, had got into them. He could do anything he chose: he would never be discovered. These two points they settled, and they went about the streets in a mood of resentful fatalism.

They talked of their ideas to the journalist in half tones, looking right and left, as though *HE* might overhear them and visit them. And though all the district was thinking of him and ready to pounce upon him, yet, so strongly had he worked upon them, that if any man in the street—say, a small man of commonplace features and form—had cried "*I* am the Monster!" would their stifled fury have broken into flood and have borne him down and engulfed him? Or would they not suddenly have seen something unearthly in that everyday face and figure, something unearthly in his everyday boots, something unearthly about his hat, something that marked him as one whom none of their weapons could alarm or pierce? And would they not momentarily have fallen back from this devil, as the devil fell back from the Cross made by the sword of Faust, and so have given him time to escape? I do not know; but so fixed was their belief in his invincibility that it is at least likely that they would have made this hesitation, had such an occasion arisen. But it never did. Today this commonplace fellow, his murder lust glutted, is still seen and observed among them as he was seen and observed all the time; but because nobody then dreamt, or now dreams, that he was what he was, they observed him then, and observe him now, as people observe a lamp-post.

Almost was their belief in his invincibility justified; for, five days after the murder of the policeman Petersen, when the experience and inspiration of the whole detective force of London were turned towards his identification and capture, he made his fourth and fifth strokes.

At nine o'clock that evening, the young newspaper man, who hung about every night until his paper was away, was strolling along Richards Lane. Richards Lane is a narrow street, partly a stall market, and partly residential. The young man was in the residential section, which carries on one side small working-class cottages, and on the other the wall of a railway goods yard. The great wall hung a blanket of shadow over the lane, and the shadow and the cadaverous outline of the now deserted market stalls gave it the appearance of a living lane that had been turned to frost in the moment between breath and death. The very lamps, that elsewhere were nimbuses of gold, had here the rigidity of gems. The journalist, feeling this message of frozen eternity, was telling himself that he was tired of the whole thing, when in one stroke the frost was broken. In the moment between one pace and another silence and darkness were racked by a high scream and through the scream a voice: "Help! help! *He's here!*"

Before he could think what movement to make, the

lane came to life. As though its invisible populace had
been waiting on that cry, the door of every cottage was
flung open, and from them and from the alleys poured
shadowy figures bent in question-mark form. For a
second or so they stood as rigid as the lamps; then a police whistle gave them direction, and the flock of shadows sloped up the street. The journalist followed them,
and others followed him. From the main street and from
surrounding streets they came, some risen from unfin-
ished suppers, some disturbed in their ease of slippers
and shirt sleeves, some stumbling on infirm limbs, and
some upright, and armed with pokers or the tools of
their trade. Here and there above the wavering cloud
of heads moved the bold helmets of policemen. In one
dim mass they surged upon a cottage whose doorway
was marked by the sergeant and two constables; and
voices of those behind urged them on with "Get in! Find
him! Run round the back! Over the wall!" and those in
front cried: "Keep back! Keep back!"

And now the fury of a mob held in thrall by unknown
peril broke loose. He was here—on the spot. Surely this
time he *could not* escape. All minds were bent upon the
cottage; all energies thrust towards its doors and windows and roof; all thought was turned upon one unknown man and his extermination. So that no one man
saw any other man. No man saw the narrow, packed
lane and the mass of struggling shadows, and all forgot
to look among themselves for the monster who never
lingered upon his victims. All forgot, indeed, that they,
by their mass crusade of vengeance, were affording him
the perfect hiding place. They saw only the house, and

heard only the rending of woodwork and the smash of glass at back and front, and the police giving orders or crying with the chase; and they pressed on.

But they found no murderer. All they found was news of murder and a glimpse of the ambulance, and for their fury there was no other object than the police themselves, who fought against this hampering of their work.

The journalist managed to struggle through to the cottage door, and to get the story from the constable stationed there. The cottage was the home of a pensioned sailor and his wife and daughter. They had been at supper, and at first it appeared that some noxious gas had smitten all three in mid-action. The daughter lay dead on the hearthrug, with a piece of bread and butter in her hand. The father had fallen sideways from his chair, leaving on his plate a filled spoon of rice pudding. The mother lay half under the table, her lap filled with the pieces of a broken cup and splashes of cocoa. But in three seconds the idea of gas was dismissed. One glance at their necks showed that this was the Strangler again; and the police stood and looked at the room and momentarily shared the fatalism of the public. They were helpless.

This was his fourth visit, making seven murders in all. He was to do, as you know, one more—and to do it that night; and then he was to pass into history as the unknown London horror, and return to the decent life that he had always led, remembering little of what he had done and worried not at all by the memory. Why did he stop? Impossible to say. Why did he begin? Impos-

sible again. It just happened like that; and if he thinks
at all of those days and nights, I surmise that he thinks
of them as we think of foolish or dirty little sins that we
committed in childhood. We say that they were not
really sins, because we were not then consciously ourselves: we had not come to realization; and we look
back at that foolish little creature that we once were,
and forgive him because he didn't know. So, I think,
with this man.

There are plenty like him. Eugene Aram, after the
murder of Daniel Clarke, lived a quiet, contented life
for fourteen years, unhaunted by his crime and unshaken in his self-esteem. Constance Kent, found Not
Guilty of the murder of her young brother, led a peaceful life for five years before she confessed. George Joseph
Smith and William Palmer lived amiably among their
fellows untroubled by fear or by remorse for their poi-
sonings and drownings. Charles Peace, at the time he
made his one unfortunate essay, had settled down into
a respectable citizen with an interest in antiques. It
happened that, after a lapse of time, these men were
discovered, but more murderers than we guess are living
decent lives today, and will die in decency, undiscovered
and unsuspected. As this man will.

But he had a narrow escape, and it was perhaps this
narrow escape that brought him to a stop. The escape
was due to an error of judgment on the part of the
journalist.

As soon as he had the full story of the affair, which
took some time, he spent fifteen minutes on the telephone, sending the story through, and at the end of the

fifteen minutes, when the stimulus of the business had left him, he felt physically tired and mentally disheveled. He was not yet free to go home; the paper would not go to press for another hour; so he turned into a bar for a drink and some sandwiches.

It was then, when he had dismissed the whole business from his mind, and was looking about the bar and admiring the landlord's taste in watch chains and his air of domination, and was thinking that the landlord of a well-conducted tavern had a more comfortable life than a newspaper man, that his mind received from nowhere a spark of light. He was not thinking about the Strangling Horrors; his mind was on his sandwich. As a public-house sandwich, it was a curiosity. The bread had been thinly cut, it was buttered, and the ham was not two months stale; it was ham as it should be. His mind turned to the inventor of this refreshment, the Earl of Sandwich, and then to George the Fourth, and then to the Georges, and to the legend of that George who was worried to know how the apple got into the apple dumpling. He wondered whether George would have been equally puzzled to know how the ham got into the ham sandwich, and how long it would have been before it occurred to him that the ham could not have got there unless somebody had put it there. He got up to order another sandwich, and in that moment a little active corner of his mind settled the affair. If there was ham in his sandwich, somebody must have put it there. If seven people had been murdered, somebody must have been there to murder them. There was no airplane or automobile that would go into a man's pocket; therefore that somebody must have escaped either by running away or standing still; and again therefore——

He was visualizing the front-page story that his paper would carry if his theory were correct, and if—a matter of conjecture—his editor had the necessary nerve to make a bold stroke, when a cry of "Time, gentlemen, please! All out!" reminded him of the hour. He got up and went out into a world of mist, broken by the ragged discs of roadside puddles and the streaming lightning of motor buses. He was certain that he had *the* story, but, even if it were proved, he was doubtful whether the policy of his paper would permit him to print it. It had one great fault. It was truth, but it was impossible truth. It rocked the foundations of everything that newspaper readers believed and that newspaper editors helped them to believe. They might believe that Turkish carpet sellers had the gift of making themselves invisible. They would not believe this.

As it happened, they were not asked to, for the story was never written. As his paper had by now gone to press, and as he was nourished by his refreshment and stimulated by his theory, he thought he might put in an extra half hour by testing that theory. So he began to look about for the man he had in mind—a man with white hair, and large white hands; otherwise an everyday figure whom nobody would look twice at. He wanted to spring his idea on this man without warning, and he was going to place himself within reach of a man armored in legends of dreadfulness and grue. This might appear to be an act of supreme courage—that one man, with no hope of immediate outside support, should place himself at the mercy of one who was holding a whole parish in terror. But it wasn't. He didn't think about the risk. He didn't think about his duty to his employers or loyalty to his paper. He was moved simply by an instinct to follow a story to its end.

He walked slowly from the tavern and crossed into Fingal Street, making for Deever Market, where he had hope of finding his man. But his journey was shortened. At the corner of Lotus Street he saw him—or a man who looked like him. This street was poorly lit, and he could see little of the man: but he *could* see white hands. For some twenty paces he stalked him; then drew level with him; and at a point where the arch of a railway crossed the street, he saw that this was his man. He approached him with the current conversational phrase of the district: "Well, seen anything of the murderer?" The man stopped to look sharply at him; then, satisfied that the journalist was not the murderer, said:

"Eh? No, nor's anybody else, curse it. Doubt if they ever will."

"I don't know. I've been thinking about them, and I've got an idea."

"So?"

"Yes. Came to me all of a sudden. Quarter of an hour ago. And I'd felt that we'd all been blind. It's been staring us in the face."

The man turned again to look at him, and the look and the movement held suspicion of this man who seemed to know so much. "Oh? Has it? Well, if you're so sure, why not give us the benefit of it?"

"I'm going to." They walked level, and were nearly at the end of the little street where it meets Deever Market, when the journalist turned casually to the man. He put a finger on his arm. "Yes, it seems to me quite simple now. But there's still one point I don't understand. One little thing I'd like to clear up. I mean the motive. Now, as man to man, tell me, Sergeant Ottermole, just *why* did you kill all those inoffensive people?"

The sergeant stopped, and the journalist stopped. There was just enough light from the sky, which held the reflected light of the continent of London, to give him a sight of the sergeant's face, and the sergeant's face was turned to him with a wide smile of such urbanity and charm that the journalist's eyes were frozen as they met it. The smile stayed for some seconds. Then said the sergeant: "Well, to tell you the truth, Mr. Newspaper Man, I don't know. I really don't know. In fact, I've been worried about it myself. But I've got an idea—just like you. Everybody knows that we can't control the workings of our minds. Don't they? Ideas come into our minds without asking. But everybody's supposed to be able to control his body. Why? Eh? We get our minds from lord-knows-where—from people who were dead hundreds of years before we were born. Mayn't we get our bodies in the same way? Our faces— our legs—our heads—they aren't completely ours. We don't make 'em. They come to us. And couldn't ideas come into our minds? Eh? Can't ideas live in nerve and muscle as well as in brain? Couldn't it be that parts of our bodies aren't really us, and couldn't ideas come into

those parts all of a sudden, like ideas come into—into"—
he shot his arms out, showing the great white-gloved
hands and hairy wrists; shot them out so swiftly to the
journalist's throat that his eyes never saw them— "into
my hands!"

The Tell-Tale Heart
by EDGAR ALLAN POE

True!—nervous—very, very dreadfully nervous I had
been and am; but why *will* you say that I am mad? The
disease had sharpened my senses—not destroyed—not
dulled them. Above all was the sense of hearing acute. I
heard all things in the heaven and in the earth. I heard
many things in hell. How, then, am I mad? Hearken!
and observe how healthily—how calmly I can tell you
the whole story.

It is impossible to say how first the idea entered my

brain; but once conceived, it haunted me day and night. Object there was none. Passion there was none. I loved the old man. He had never wronged me. He had never given me insult. For his gold I had no desire. I think it was his eye! yes, it was this! He had the eye of a vulture —a pale blue eye, with a film over it. Whenever it fell upon me, my blood ran cold; and so by degrees—very gradually—I made up my mind to take the life of the old man, and thus rid myself of the eye forever.

Now this is the point. You fancy me mad. Madmen know nothing. But you should have seen *me*. You should have seen how wisely I proceeded—with what caution— with what foresight—with what dissimulation I went to work! I was never kinder to the old man than during the whole week before I killed him. And every night, about midnight, I turned the latch of his door and opened it— oh so gently! And then, when I had made an opening sufficient for my head, I put in a dark lantern, all closed, closed, so that no light shone out, and then I thrust in my head. Oh, you would have laughed to see how cunningly I thrust it in! I moved it slowly—very, very slowly, so that I might not disturb the old man's sleep. It took me an hour to place my whole head within the opening so far that I could see him as he lay upon his bed. Ha!—would a madman have been so wise as this? And then, when my head was well in the room, I undid the lantern cautiously—oh, so cautiously—cautiously (for the hinges creaked)—I undid it just so much that a single thin ray fell upon the vulture eye. And this I did for seven long nights—every night just at midnight— but I found the eye always closed; and so it was impossible to do the work; for it was not the old man who vexed me, but his Evil Eye. And every morning, when the day broke, I went boldly into the chamber, and spoke courageously to him, calling him by name in a hearty tone, and inquiring how he had passed the night. So you see he would have been a very profound old man indeed to suspect that every night, just at twelve, I looked in upon him while he slept.

Upon the eighth night I was more than usually cautious in opening the door. A watch's minute hand moves more quickly than did mine. Never before that night had I *felt* the extent of my own powers—of my sagacity. I could scarcely contain my feelings of triumph. To think that there I was, opening the door, little by little, and he not even to dream of my secret deeds or thoughts. I fairly chuckled at the idea; and perhaps he heard me; for he moved on the bed suddenly, as if startled. Now you may think that I drew back—but no. His room was as black as pitch with the thick darkness (for the shutters were close fastened, through fear of robbers), and so I knew that he could not see the opening of the door, and I kept pushing it on steadily, steadily.

I had my head in, and was about to open the lantern, when my thumb slipped upon the tin fastening, and the old man sprang up in bed, crying out—"Who's there?"

I kept quite still and said nothing. For a whole hour I did not move a muscle, and in the meantime I did not hear him lie down. He was still sitting up in the bed listening; just as I have done, night after night, hearkening to the death watches in the wall.

Presently I heard a slight groan, and I knew it was

the groan of mortal terror. It was not a groan of pain or of grief—oh, no!—it was the low stifled sound that arises from the bottom of the soul when overcharged with awe. I knew the sound well. Many a night, just at midnight, when all the world slept, it has welled up from my own bosom, deepening, with its dreadful echo, the terrors that distracted me. I say I knew it well. I knew what the old man felt, and pitied him, although I chuckled at heart. I knew that he had been lying awake ever since the first slight noise, when he had turned in the bed. His fears had been ever since growing upon him. He had been trying to fancy them causeless, but could not. He had been saying to himself, "It is nothing but the wind in the chimney—it is only a mouse crossing the floor," or "it is merely a cricket which has made a single chirp." Yes, he had been trying to comfort himself with these suppositions: but he had found all in vain. *All in vain;* because Death, in approaching him, had stalked with his black shadow before him, and enveloped the victim. And it was the mournful influence of the un-perceived shadow that caused him to feel—although he neither saw nor heard—to *feel* the presence of my head within the room.

When I had waited a long time, very patiently, with-out hearing him lie down, I resolved to open a little—a very, very little crevice in the lantern. So I opened it—you cannot imagine how stealthily, stealthily—until, at length, a simple dim ray, like the thread of the spider, shot out from the crevice and fell full upon the vulture eye.

It was open—wide, wide open—and I grew furious as

I gazed upon it. I saw it with perfect distinctness—all a dull blue, with a hideous veil over it that chilled the very marrow in my bones; but I could see nothing else of the old man's face or person: for I had directed the ray as if by instinct, precisely upon the spot.

And have I not told you that what you mistake for madness is but over-acuteness of the senses? Now, I say, there came to my ears a low, dull, quick sound, such as a watch makes when enveloped in cotton. I knew *that* sound well, too. It was the beating of the old man's heart. It increased my fury, as the beating of a drum stimulates the soldier into courage.

But even yet I refrained and kept still. I scarcely breathed. I held the lantern motionless. Meantime the hellish tattoo of the heart increased. It grew quicker and quicker, and louder and louder every instant. The old man's terror *must* have been extreme! It grew louder, I say, louder every moment!—do you mark me well? I have told you that I am nervous: so I am. And now at the dead hour of the night, amid the dreadful silence of that old house, so strange a noise as this excited me to uncontrollable terror. Yet, for some minutes longer I refrained and stood still. But the beating grew louder, louder! I thought the heart must burst. And now a new anxiety seized me—the sound would be heard by a neighbor! The old man's hour had come! With a loud yell, I threw open the lantern and leaped into the room. He shrieked once—once only. In an instant I dragged him to the floor, and pulled the heavy bed over him. I then smiled gaily, to find the deed so far done. But, for many minutes, the heart beat on with a muffled sound.

This, however, did not vex me; it would not be heard through the wall. At length it ceased. The old man was dead. I removed the bed and examined the corpse. Yes, he was stone, stone dead. I placed my hand upon the heart and held it there many minutes. There was no pulsation. He was stone dead. His eye would trouble me no more.

If still you think me mad, you will think so no longer when I describe the wise precautions I took for the concealment of the body. The night waned, and I worked hastily, but in silence. First of all I dismembered the corpse. I cut off the head and the arms and the legs.

I then took up three planks from the flooring of the chamber, and deposited all between the scantlings. I then replaced the boards so cleverly, so cunningly, that no human eye—not even *his*—could have detected any thing wrong. There was nothing to wash out—no stain of any kind—no blood spot whatever. I had been too wary for that. A tub had caught all—ha! ha!

When I had made an end of these labors, it was four o'clock—still dark as midnight. As the bell sounded the hour, there came a knocking at the street door. I went down to open it with a light heart, for what had I *now* to fear? There entered three men who introduced themselves, with perfect suavity, as officers of the police. A shriek had been heard by a neighbor during the night; suspicion of foul play had been aroused; information had been lodged at the police office, and they (the officers) had been deputed to search the premises.

I smiled, for *what* had I to fear? I bade the gentlemen welcome. The shriek, I said, was my own in a dream.

The old man, I mentioned, was absent in the country. I took my visitors all over the house. I bade them search —search *well*. I led them, at length, to *his* chamber. I showed them his treasures, secure, undisturbed. In the enthusiasm of my confidence, I brought chairs into the room, and desired them *here* to rest from their fatigues, while I myself, in the wild audacity of my perfect triumph, placed my own seat upon the very spot beneath which reposed the corpse of the victim.

The officers were satisfied. My *manner* had convinced them. I was singularly at ease. They sat, and while I answered cheerily, they chatted of familiar things. But, ere long, I felt myself geting pale and wished them gone. My head ached, and I fancied a ringing in my ears: but still they sat and still chatted. The ringing became more distinct: it continued and became more distinct: I talked more freely to get rid of the feeling: but it continued and gained definiteness—until, at length, I found that the noise was *not* within my ears.

No doubt I now grew *very* pale; but I talked more fluently, and with a heightened voice. Yet the sound increased—and what could I do? It was *a low, dull, quick sound—much such a sound as a watch makes when enveloped in cotton*. I gasped for breath—and yet the officers heard it not. I talked more quickly—more vehemently; but the noise steadily increased. I arose and argued about trifles, in a high key and with violent gesticulations; but the noise steadily increased. Why *would* they not be gone? I paced the floor to and fro with heavy strides, as if excited to fury by the observations of the men—but the noise steadily increased. Oh God!

what *could* I do? I foamed—I raved—I swore! I swung the chair upon which I had been sitting, and grated it upon the boards, but the noise arose over all and continually increased. It grew louder—louder—*louder!* And still the men chatted pleasantly, and smiled. Was it possible they heard not? Almighty God!—no, no! They heard!—they suspected!—they *knew!*—they were making a mockery of my horror!—this I thought, and this I think. But anything was better than this agony! Anything was more tolerable than this derision! I could bear those hypocritical smiles no longer! I felt that I must scream or die! and now—again!—hark! louder! louder! louder! *louder!*

"Villains!" I shrieked, "dissemble no more! I admit the deed!—tear up the planks! Here, here!—it is the beating of his hideous heart!"

About the Editor

Robert Arthur had a lifelong interest in ghosts, haunts, demons, dragons, witchcraft, and magic. Once he lived in an old bat-infested house, where the bats would swoop around his head as he typed—just the right atmosphere for a writer of ghost and mystery stories.

By the time of his death in 1969, Mr. Arthur had written more than 1000 magazine stories, 500 radio scripts, and at least 75 television scripts. He was a story consultant and writer for the "Alfred Hitchcock Presents" mystery anthologies, and also wrote for Boris Karloff and others. His numerous books for children include anthologies of mystery and suspense stories, such as *Mystery and More Mystery* and *Spies and More Spies,* and ten titles in the popular "Alfred Hitchcock and The Three Investigators" mystery series. Mr. Arthur's work twice won him an Edgar Award (the mystery-writing equivalent of the "Oscar").

Mr. Arthur was born on Corregidor Island in the Philippines, where his father was a colonel in the U.S. Army. He began writing as a teenager and was first published when he was 16. After graduation from the University of Michigan with honors in literature, he worked as a magazine editor in New York City before turning to free-lance writing.